Copyright © November 2014, Ginger Branch
Edited by FastWriter247and Valerie Decal
Cover Designed by Angie Zambrano
ISBN: 978-0-9863424-1-7

Warning: This book is intended for adults 18+ only. It contains scenes of violence, rape, profanity, death, consensual sex between m/f and dubious consent between m/m.

<u>Dedication & Thanks</u>

For my Mom - who is my best friend and confident! You taught me, and pushed me on occasion, okay a great many occasions, to reach for the stars. This first one is just for you.

With special thanks to all my beta readers Brittney Estrada, Cindi Holley, Linda Scott, Nicole Saph Marheine, Lee A. Weems, Vicki Grewal, Janice Green, Ed Decal and Sean Barry. You are an author's superhero! Thank you very much for your insights.

KNIGHT IN SHINING ALIEN?

BY GINGER BRANCH

Table of Contents

Prologue

In a war that lasted for a thousand years, the Quarnon family finally managed to decimate a large portion of their enemies ships and push their hated enemy the Krakill's away from their planet. Instead of celebrating their victory, they found themselves on the brink of extinction. Knowing that the Krakill's wanted to steal their women for reproduction, they had hid them away deep in their mountains with two thousand warriors to guard them. All they found upon their return was a cavern full of dead warriors and severely hurt, dying, traumatized or missing women. The women who remained told of the horrors visited upon them. That when the Krakill where finished with them, they either executed their sisters or injected them with chemicals which burned and hurt their bellies. Discovering that the Krakill's had destroyed their reproduction capabilities, the Athrian's, led by King Arbus Marrek Quarnon, turned the throne and planet over to his son and vowed to wipe the Krakill from existence. He took half of his battle destroyers, filled them with warriors, scientists, mechanics, and other personnel and told them to search out every star and moon for two things. First, seek out the fleeing hoard and kill all that they found, while searching for the Krakill's home world, so that they could destroy the evil at its source. The second task was just as important. Seek out any species that they could successfully breed with to try to preserve their race. The remainder of their race guarded against any further return of their enemy and prayed to the Goddess for a miracle. Will she hear their prayers and guide the future king of Athria, Jarrek, to his destiny? Will he manage to win her heart?

1.

Kidnapped by Aliens?

Is this a joke?

If a "do-over" were an actual thing, I would reconsider the idea of getting out of bed this morning and call into work with a serious case of swine flu. Awake and up before six that morning, showered and dressed by six fifteen in faded denim and a peasant blouse of emerald green. It looked like a medieval gown, with elastic just under the breasts and above the elbows, leaving the rest of the fabric loose and free to hang down. Black Justin lace up boots with the fringed tongue completed the wardrobe for the day and I was ready to head off for breakfast.

Normally, I hit the snooze button about twelve times and talk myself into getting up, but this morning I never even touched the snooze button and was perkily awake. I should have figured that was a bad omen. I am never bouncy and rarely perky, I am sarcastic and even "bitchy" a good percent of the time. Why I started the day so happy and bouncy I will probably never know, but I did and went merrily on my way to work singing along to the radio the whole way.

I work alone as a property manager for a storage company, and now that we just entered the fall season, with winter coming quickly behind, the days are slowing and quiet. Which, honestly I prefer, as then I don't have to deal with a lot of my fellow bitchy people out in the big bad world. The smell, however, when I walked in the door was the most disgusting thing ever. It smelled like a four-day corpse during the height of a 115-degree summer where the air conditioner is broken, with a helping of just sprayed skunk and something that rolled in a very full septic tank. At first, I just thought that maybe something got stuck and died under the house or in the vents- it had happened at the beginning of summer. As I walked to the kitchen area, the smell just got worse.

I held my breath, hoping that the smell would dissipate a little when I opened the back door, but as I passed the hall, a tall figure came at me and I screamed at the top of my lungs and swung my purse at what looked like twigs coming at me. When my purse connected to whatever the twig looking things were, I found myself nauseous and blinded by a weird flashing strobe light. When I blinked a few times, I found myself lying on a mat in a cage. Seriously, a freaking metal bar cage.

Now, I'm not someone that will cry at the drop of the hat, scared of confrontation. I am usually the one doing the yelling and confronting with sarcasm at the ready, but I honestly think that I began to have a little emotional melt down at this point. I went the gamut from thinking that maybe this was all a nightmare and I would wake up in a minute and be relieved it was over, to knowing it was real and not understanding how I could believe it was real. I felt as though I was going crazy.

I was completely ready for the big strong orderlies to come in with the straight jacket and send me off with happy drugs to a little padded room.

I paced back and forth for a while in that cage; every now and again pinching myself to make sure, I was still in the real! It probably took me an hour to calm myself down and take a good look around me. I was hoping that whatever had put me in this cage- I still was not going to say alien at this point, not even inside my own head- would think I had the intelligence of a gerbil and it would be easy to escape.

That was what my cage reminded me of, something you would find in a pet store for a rabbit or guinea pig. Guinea pig was not a thought I should have had, so I scolded myself… "Bad thought, don't go there."

The bars were about three inches apart and about two inches thick with a horizontal bar about every four feet. It held a padded cushion on one side of the floor with a light blanket and on the other side was a round hole where a huge bottle of water hung upside down. It steadily dripped water that would run down the little hole. I figured it was probably the toilet, shower and water source all in one. Gross! I debated on whether to call out for help and see if anything else was out there, but the more I thought about it the more I scared my own damn self.

Where was the knight in shining armor to rescue me? I practically snorted myself into passing out I laughed so hard at that thought. Okay, I was also maybe still in emotional freak out land. So sue me. You get kidnapped by a weird twig armed thing, and then see how you handle it.

Calm again, I tried to move on. I was on my own in figuring out how to get home. Outside my little slice of heaven, there were stacks and rows of cages. It looked like a huge cavern from my vantage point of the second floor of row Crazy town as I named my humble abode. I could not see into any of the cages. It looked dark out there, just shapes of cages and little lights that lit a corridor between my row and the one across from me.

The problem was I could see no door or opening on my little cage. The hole in the floor was no bigger than my closed fist. I found nothing that looked remotely like a lock or way out. Great, just what I was looking for, a hopeless feeling. I sank down onto the little padded mattress. Where were the pom-poms so I could shake them as I chanted, "Rock 'em, sock 'em, knock 'em down. You are so going to die. Goooooo team Death!"

As I sat there being snarky with myself, a little ray of hope and sunshine broke through. If whatever or whoever had wanted me dead, then presumably I would be so. Since not wanting me dead would likely lead to feedings and maybe taking me out of this cage at some point, I needed to get smart and figure out how I would take advantage of that time. I grabbed my purse and started rifling through the contents.

I got into carrying a big purse from my Mom, who always held to the tenant of, "You never know what you may need." I pretty much have everything and the kitchen sink with me at all times. My Kindle, small ratchet set, small screwdriver set with Phillips, flat and hexagon heads, Swiss army knife with a corkscrew opener. I have straws, travel shower set, a manicure kit, a handful of wet-ones wipes, some plastic sporks, eight packets of energy crystal light in peach mango flavor (the best and only flavor in my personal opinion) and even a vast array of condiments. There was a small make-up case with perfume and jewelry. I had a decent selection of medicines and feminine hygiene products. The usual suspects of brush, comb, germx and some lotion finished the contents. I laid out all the items in rows to go over my supplies and see if anything was helpful. The cell phone had no service, I tried that as soon as my brain connected and I remembered I had them.

At the bottom of my purse I found my little jewelry making and repair kit. Tada! Eureka! I wanted to giggle and dance around the room. The kit has some needle nose pliers and best of all, wire cutters! I quickly threw everything back in my purse except the wire cutters and needle nose pliers. I pulled my purse across me like a messenger bag and stepped up to the bars. I was not quite sure this would work, but better to try and fail than to sit on your ass and let who knows what happen to you.

I cannot tell you how long I worked on cutting into the bars before I heard some noise coming towards me, but it felt like several hours. I had some blisters and torn a couple of nails, but I could see progress was being made; I had about seven bars almost completely cut through.

The swishy sound of fabric dragging on the ground and weird jibberish came into my hearing, so I quickly stashed my tools before looking down. Three tall lizard-like aliens with skin like an alligator with protruding ridges walked down the corridor, two of them dragging another captive. He looked huge even from my vantage point. At least seven feet tall with deep red skin, long black hair, and muscles on top of muscles, but mostly still humanoid in appearance. He had on a very form-fitting suit in black with heavy biker boots. At this point, I don't think I could deny aliens had abducted me. Then there was that remembered stench from walking into my office. These creatures, whatever they were, they could not have an olfactory sense. They would have shot themselves long ago and did the universe a favor by going extinct.

I was surprised that it only took two of the creatures to drag Mr. Red Alien. They had very thin arms, with spines running down the back of each arm. On the top of their heads, more spines ran all the way down to a tail that helped them stay upright. They had big, ball-like rounded eyes on the top of their almost triangular heads and when they talked to each other out of a wide slit for a mouth with no lips, they showed a set of razor sharp teeth. I could not see ears, but they could have been flat against their skull. They were making weird thrrrwwping tweets in various bass, baritone and alto chords between one another that I assumed was a language.

They let go of Mr. Red Alien and shot him with the same twig arms they had used on me. So, I guess I wasn't abducted by a tree, nice to know. He disappeared and reappeared inside the cage across from me on the bottom floor. The cages above him and next to him, all along the row also lit up briefly with more of the red aliens as occupants. It looked like they had captured quite a few of the red guys. I started wondering why I was apparently alone in my captivity, but Mr. Red got company. Then I completely forgot about it as one of the stink men, the one who had not helped carry the other prisoner, walked over to my side and climbed up to look in at me.

I couldn't tell if he was looking me over as a delicacy that he wanted to eat or if I was some science experiment, but I tried to back as far away as I could get. The smell alone had me ready to hurl. How can you fight something that makes you want to vomit before you can get close enough to kill it? Twenty feet was excessively close for my stomach's sake. I held my breath and hoped they would not kill me or take away my stuff. I don't think that he noticed I was cutting the bars, but I didn't want to take the chance that he would. Especially as one of his four claw hands were inches from where I had cut. I put my arm across my nose and tried to breath in the smell of my perfume on my clothes. Unfortunately all I could smell was the nasty alien. Wondering if I was about to be killed pissed me off and there went my brain to mouth filter.

I put my arm down, stepped forward a few feet, leaned forward, looked that bubble-headed jerk in the eye, and said, "Can you go the fuck away before I vomit? You really stink! Have you even heard of soap and water? Either kill me and get it over with, or go the fuck away! Seriously! I can't take your disgusting smell anymore." I held my breath again as I waited to see what would happen.

Mr. Stinky chirped and tweeted, - which if you wondered, may sound all cute and cuddly, but is downright scary- and then a long, forked tongue came out of his slit of a mouth and licked up my cheek. My stomach dropped a little more. I had not thought of that. I don't speak alien, but being looked at as if I was a new toy to be undressed and played with and having some creepy thing lick you, ugh. Well, let's just say that some things don't need a translator, they are universally understood.

"Buddy there is no way on my or any other planet that I will let you rape me. You can just get that thought right out of your tiny little mind." I put my hand in my purse and came out with what I hoped was my Swiss knife, but turned out to be hand sanitizer. I poured some in my hand and flung it at him. It sizzled on his scaly skin and he jerked back. "I will melt your skin right off your face, you creep! Back off! My pussy has razor blades inside that will bite your tiny little dick off!" I screamed at him as I tried to push my body through the bars on the other side of the cage.

Mr. Stinky alien raised his hand to his smoking face and then did the scariest thing yet. His lip-less mouth tilted up in a parody of a smile and then he opened that slit, showing many scary teeth and with his forked tongue, the word "Sssssoooon" came out. I prayed to all the Gods and Goddesses of the universe that he was wrong.

As soon as he left I went back to work on the cage with a vengeance. I had all kinds of new reasons to get the heck out of dodge. My mind kept up a running commentary of stupid thoughts and phrases along the lines of "Why me? What the heck? Have you slipped off the deep end and forgot to tell me? And how could they want to rape me?" I am not ugly, but I am not Miss America or Miss Universe. I am a size sixteen on a good day and eighteen on a bad day. I am jiggly and soft with a rounded, pudgy tummy that has not seen crunches since elementary school. Sure, I have big boobs and hips, but J-Lo and Kim Kardashian I am not. I have big gray eyes and long brown hair with blonde highlights. I hit the average lottery for height at five feet five inches. That is it, Hailey Rose Edmondson in the flesh. Nothing spectacular, well except to my mom. I had to stop thinking of my mom. I would break down into a blubbery mess. No one would even think to look for me until dinnertime. What would this do to my mom's health? "Oh God," I moaned. I tried to keep my mind focused on being pissed and getting free, but trying to get through each section of bars was a process that felt like an eternity. I did not know what kind of period I was looking at for stink man's return. Then a loud moan came from the opposite side. Looks like Red was waking up.

"Shivak loch croin!" Red shouted. I figured that translated to son of a bitch in alien speak. He had the most heavy and seductive accent. My skin got goose bumps and my panties damp just from the sound of his voice. If we were on earth, I would think that he was Scottish with a thick brogue. The thrill that went through me listening to him curse made me want to get closer to him and at the same time to hide myself away. My pussy should not be slick and swollen, turned on by some red-skinned alien.

He glanced up and our eyes met. His obsidian and silver eyes, even from a distance, mesmerized me for a moment before I could really look at him. His long black hair was actually more of a Mohawk with the sides bare, the top was shorter than the back and was wider than I was used to seeing from the Mohawk hairstyle on earth by several inches.

His brows arched beautifully over those mesmerizing eyes. His nose was a sharp blade only softening at the end to give it a more roman appearance. His lips begged me to trace them with my fingers and tongue. He stole the breath from my body. The muscles on that man had me ready to start nibbling my way down his long body to discover just how hard he really was.

I had never seen a man that was both masculine and beautiful. He made Matthew McConaughey look like a pre-pubescent boy, and he is, well he was, my go to man for guaranteed orgasms. I forced myself to look away and break the spell he had on me and moved back into the shadows.

I had disappeared into the shadows not a moment too soon, as Red's fellow captives began to wake and call out in their language for one another. I could not be sure if he shouted "Faval!" at them or me. I slowly inched back to the bars, compelled to watch Red and listen to his voice. It soon became clear that he was the captain or leader, as when he spoke they all listened and answered accordingly. I watched as he closed his eyes and took a deep breath. The silver in his eyes blazed when he opened them again and once more, I was mesmerized.

He spoke several fast words and I heard the rest of his crew gasp as a group. What the heck? I watched as across from me another red person turned up his head and sniffed the air. I figured he was trying to figure out how close the stinky aliens were, so I was shocked when he whipped his head in my direction.

I immediately looked down towards Red, looking for some type of protection. He was looking back at me with an intense look upon his face. When I looked around, I saw that all of the red guys were looking at me with the same intense look upon their faces.

It was unsettling to say the least. I swallowed the lump that had appeared in my throat and looked back to Red. "Hi ya'll."

2.

I'm Not your Cordisa!

Jarrek T'el Quarnon, Commander of the battle cruiser Sh'dow al D'th and Prince of the planet Athria came back to consciousness with a loud groan and a curse already forming on his lips, which he immediately let loose. He slowly sat up and reached to touch the back of his head. Silently he thanked the gods there was no blood, although he continued to verbally curse at his hated enemy Varill. Sorry bastard had actually found a little luck and had managed to capture him.

Why was he still alive? He was male so he could not contribute anything viable for procreation and he was not a good candidate in their search for edible protein with specific enzymes, so what could his old enemy be thinking? He thought that he would finally get a chance to kill Varill just outside of a small blue and white planet and had commanded his ship to cloak itself behind a large planet with rings and moons while he and a select group of his guard took a small shuttle on a stealth mission to board the Krakill vessel. In dealing with the Krakill over the years, he had found that surprise and small concentrated teams usually managed to kill most of them.

The Krakill advanced in DNA manipulation and other sciences could not create better technology for space travel or war. It was as if they could concentrate on only two things, procreation and war. They did not even get to enjoy it either. They only used females to harvest their eggs. Then they jerked themselves off and fertilized the ova in a dish before inserting it into an incubator-egg. They had about two days to harvest an egg from a female and fertilize it before the outer layers of their egg hardened too much to introduce the mixed DNA. Not to say they did not enjoy hurting a woman, but no penetration was required for them to procreate. What a waste. Females were soft and beautiful and smelled so good. They had such lovely breasts to suck on, pinch, and squeeze. A pussy that was warm and tight and would milk and squeeze him until he could not hold back a second longer.

Jarrek curbed his thoughts before they made his shaft rise. There would be time later to fantasize about finding a woman. First, he had to figure out what Varill was trying to accomplish by keeping him alive. Well, he would when his head quit throbbing. It was messing up all his senses. His cock was trying to rise and he would have sworn he smelled his mate, except the Goddess of life had not blessed him or any Athrian with such a thing for the last six thousand years. They were a slowly dying race, looking about the galaxy for a compatible species to breed with; they were also trying to kill off the Krakill race. If they were destined to die, they wanted to leave the universe a safer place.

Looking up, he froze as he caught sight of the most amazingly beautiful and exotic woman he had ever seen. Her eyes were the color of a Jabir's egg. Her skin was a shimmering brown and olive tone. Her hair was long and thick and the exact color of the soil, rich with the minerals and nutrients needed in springtime, abundant with veins of the life giving sun throughout. He was unable to see all of her, but her breasts were large and bountiful. He could not wait to taste them. She was a goddess come to life.

For an instant, he thought that maybe the hit to his head had been too hard and he was hallucinating, especially as she moved away from the bars and back into the cage where he could no longer see her. He tried to shout out for her to wait, but it seemed like he was not alone in his captivity. More and more of his men called out to one another. It seems that Varill had managed to capture his entire guard. Well, no matter. It would make it that much easier to escape from here if they all combined their energies. Then he could find out if that vision of pulchritude was real by pulling her into his arms for a few mind-drugging kisses.

He ran through the roll call, making sure each warrior could be accounted for, before he then satisfied his own need and took another deep breath. He wanted to verify what his soul already knew. Her scent was so unique and delicious. His mouth watered. His cock went from soft to hard and painful in a microsec. She really was his mate. The Goddess had given him a mate! Quickly, he told his crew. The urgency to escape and kill Varill had just multiplied by a googolplex. He heard their collective gasps and indrawn breaths, trying to verify his words. Not because they doubted him, but because such a thing was so inconceivable that, they felt compelled to verify his words for themselves. It was hard to fathom that they were finally going to know what a mate could scent like.

There were plenty of pleasure houses throughout the galaxy for warriors, pirates, trader's, even criminals. They had several such places on their home world of Athria, as they paid very well and looked upon the women not as whores, but princesses. Females capable of mating and breeding with the males of their species were extinct, a myth, a hopeless dream. There were only five thousand of their own women alive on their planet. Each warrior present had given up the idea of finding their mate and concentrated on taking out as many of their hated enemy as possible before joining the Goddess in death. That their Prince should find a female mate was a surprise.

Jarrek kept his eyes trained on the female, his Jabir minka or "my little bird", as she looked around at his men. When she looked back down at him, he was sorry to see her look so frightened. Once he got her out of that cage, he would make sure that she knew that she was his to protect and she never needed to be afraid again. Any one of his men would give his life to keep her safe. It would be his honor to spend every minute devoted to her safety and happiness.

At her small greeting, he had to frown. What language was that? He had a cornucopia of languages that he was fluent in, several more that he could get by with his basic understanding of, but success in universal translators had been on the market now for the last few years. He had purchased them for all of his crew and even sent several crates back to his father, King Cybrus. They may be a dying race, but they were men.

New technology had always fascinated his father and he knew he would enjoy playing with one and finding out how it worked. He would also challenge his scientists to improve upon the work by chastising them for not figuring out how to create them in the first place. He was going to need to get her to keep talking so that his implant could decipher her language and translate it for him. Although that did not seem to be a problem as she continued speaking, without the need for breath apparently.

Hailey saw Red's frown and wondered for a moment if she had said something that translated to something offensive in his language. Giving herself a mental shrug, as she could not help it if their languages were so different that one small word would offend she kept going and said, "I really hope that you aren't frowning at me because I dared to speak to you. I mean I was only trying to be friendly. I'm southern. We almost have to be friendly. It's like the religion of the south. Well I'm currently a Texan. I was born what they call a Yankee, but I have been in Texas since I was like twelve. I hope you are the nice kind of alien. I really would prefer it if you were the nice kind of aliens, instead of eat your brains kind of aliens, you know what I mean? Ugh, of course you don't know what I mean. The chances of you being able to understand my language have to be a million to one. No, probably bigger than that, like a trillion to one. Well, I don't care. I actually feel a little more like myself now that I am talking aloud to ya'll. I wonder why I didn't think of this earlier. I could have sung some songs while I worked on trying to break out of this prison. Like Jailhouse rock, from the King of Pop, Mr. Elvis Presley. Maybe something a little more today, ummm…nope can't think of any prison songs. Some country maybe or I love the band Three Days Grace. Hey, you don't know what kind of alien thing kidnapped us, do you? Ooh, and are they as evil as I think they are? Do you know why that one dude licked my cheek? He wasn't trying to see if I would taste good barbequed, was he? Why did he kidnap me in the first place? Why did he kidnap you? Where did he kidnap you from? Y' all haven't been to my planet before, have you? 'Cuz I have to say, I used to think those people that claimed they had been kidnapped by aliens, had really just gotten a hold of some real good moonshine. I may have to apologize to them if I ever get back home. I'm really worried that Mr. Stinky is going to come back soon, so while it was real nice talking to you, unless you can magic us all out of here, I need to get back to trying to break out."

Taking out her wire cutters and needle nose pliers, she started talking to Red and the others while she worked again. "I really think I may be close. I will leave you my tools so you can break out too, but I have to hide. I just don't think that I want to be around when ugly gets back. I'm sure as hell not going to wait for him to rape me and I will not sit around to see if he does want to barbeque me. No thanks. Ha! Got you, you sweet sugar you." So saying she used her needle nose pliers to help her bend down two of the ten bars she had managed to saw through away from her. Once that was accomplished, she judged the opening itself. It would be a tight fit, but she would make it work. She started to bend the other bars towards her.

Packing up her tools, she used her own weight to help bend the other eight bars back as far as she could. She then pushed her purse through the opening and hung it on the two bars she had bent outside of the cage. Taking a deep breath and saying a small prayer she began climbing up the bars. She was going to go out of here feet first.

The red people went crazy, and whispered shouts came from up and down the row. She still couldn't understand what the heck they were saying, but she got the gist. However, if they kept up the noise it would bring Mr. Stinky back sooner rather than later and she wanted to be gone before that occurred, so with a stern look at Mr. Red and a "Shh! Do you want mister stinky, ugly alien to come back?" she resumed her climb. Since he was the leader, he could tell the rest of his people to shut it up.

Going headfirst only made sense to her as she could drag herself or hop if she broke a leg, but if she went headfirst she could break her neck. Of course, she was going to be very careful not to break anything. The idea was to find a way to hide and escape.

Hailey threaded both feet through the opening and then sat on the edge to get her balance and some advantage to help turn her onto her stomach. She slowly rolled over until her legs were straight out behind her and she balanced on her stomach. Lowering her legs, she looked for something to help hold her weight and control the balance.

There were vertical bars running about every four feet that helped. Reaching under herself with one hand, she pushed her upper body up while reaching above herself to grab a bar. Ducking under the opening, she was now standing outside her little cage. She carefully slipped her purse across her body, then slowly bent her knees, and walked herself down the bar as far as she could. When she lowered her legs down to the next vertical section, she took another deep breath and started the process all over again. It was just letting gravity take hold in a slow controlled slide. Four vertical sections later, Hailey touched solid ground then did a little booty shake in victory. She then turned around to keep her promise.

Turning around to face Red, she took just a moment to study him. Now that she was just a few feet away from him, his sheer size overwhelmed her. Thinking that he must be at least seven feet tall, then standing almost next to seven feet tall, were worlds apart in the feelings it engendered. She felt small and vulnerable. One feeling she quite liked, being an overweight woman, she rarely felt small, but vulnerable was not a feeling she liked at all. That feeling would quickly piss her off.

Hailey quickly pulled out the needle nose pliers and wire cutters then held them out to Mr. Red. The bars width may have been helpful to Hailey, but regrettably, Red was going to have to open a bunch of bars before he could escape. Feeling safe from any attempts to grab a hold of her, Hailey got closer to the bars than she would have normally thought wise.

"Here are the tools I promised. Good luck on getting free." She pushed the tools inside the cage. She took a minute and tried to memorize the overall look of him. If she ever got free or even found some privacy for a little while, she was going to use him to replace Mr. McConaughey. He was the sexiest, the most masculine, yummy man she had ever seen. Looking at him this close had her pussy gushing. She felt like she could almost drown someone in the juice her pussy was creating. That saying, "I want to eat him with a spoon," applied here, except. "I don't want a spoon. My tongue would work just fine," she told him.

"What would your tongue work on? Why would it work at all? It is in your mouth." Jarrek asked. Sometime during her very long talking, his translator had kicked in and started translating what she was saying. She had a very odd way of speaking and many of her words ran together so that it took a little effort on his part to separate them and try to understand her meaning. He had just managed to decipher her last words when she started her ridiculous climb out the hole she had made. He wanted to shout at her to stop, but was afraid that if he managed to say anything it would only scare her and make her fall.

His men had protested as well. When they escaped he was going to spank her ass bright red. He felt as though his heart muscle was going to seize up. Watching that backside view as she slowly made her way down had given him amble time to picture it lying across his lap for discipline. The little shake she had given it when she was finally on the ground had made his already painful cock, swell further, making him moan a little. He was about to explode like some youngling with his first rise. His body's reaction to her look was visceral. When she had held out her strange objects but continued to run her eyes over his body, it felt as though she was searing his skin, the very fluid in his bones.

"On you." She answered absently. Still trying to catalog the ways his muscles moved as he shifted. Then the fact that he spoke in English, and that she had answered him registered. Hailey felt her face heat up and she finished shoving the tools into his cage and backed up quickly. "What the heck?"

Hailey was surprised to hear him speak English. "What's wrong with you? I have been speaking for the better part of an hour and not once have you attempted to speak with me or answer any of my questions. If you didn't know the answer, you could have just said so." She pushed the hair from her eyes, rolled them and continued.

"Sweet baby Jesus, it just figures that I am kidnapped by aliens and the male of the species still keeps their mouths shut. Apparently, the silent type is everywhere. That's just great." Hailey ended on a sigh. So embarrassed that she wanted to melt in the floor, she pushed her shoulders back and held her head up high. "You can figure out on your own how to use the tools. You're male, so it's not like you would have listened to my instructions in the first place." Turning away from the direction that Mr. Stinky went Hailey took off down the corridor. It was time to stop drooling over sexy red aliens and escape.

Hailey only made it fifty yards before she smacked into a very solid wall of muscle, and let out an audible oomph. She looked up the wall of muscles and into eyes of obsidian and silver. She felt her heart skip a beat and then begin again in double time. What kind of spell was he able to weave over her?

"Are you made of bricks? That hurt." Hailey said before she it registered that he had been inside a cage only a second ago. "Wait! How did you get out?"

"That is not important my little bird. Here are your small sticks. You can put them in your bag. My men are securing the way out of here. I do not know why Varill has not killed us yet, but I do not have time to find out what he has planned, as I would prefer we escape now." Pulling her up against his chest so that he could look at her beautiful face he quickly strode down the corridor after his men.

"Look Red, I don't know who you think you are, but I am not going with you. You can put me down right now." Hailey tried pushing against his chest and wiggling out of his hold, but it was like trying to move a mountain with a feather. She punched him in the chest and only managed to hurt her hand. "I will hurt you if you don't put me down right this fucking instant!"

"Not Red, Jarrek. My name is Jarrek, and you are not hurting me. You are too small and soft to hurt me. I could carry you for hours you are so light. We must leave here now before Varill comes back.

"Okay, that is it Mister! You can't say I didn't warn you." She had just about enough. To make fun of her weight was not something that she could tolerate. Hailey's emotional trauma was rising again, and like her patience, was at the end of the rope. She kicked him solidly between his legs.

Hailey expected a sudden, harsh drop when Jarrek fell to the floor in agony. What she didn't expect was that she would be the one to scream. Her foot connected with something that felt as solid as steel. "Ahhhh" she started, but Jarrek placed his hand over her mouth to contain her scream. She knew something had broken.

"I am sorry my little bird, I know you are in pain, but I will have you healed in just a moment. Please be patient as we wait for my men to give the signal. We are just outside of the corridor where we have hidden our shuttle." Jarrek asked as he watched the tears fall down her beautiful cheeks.

He was extremely proud of her for trying to fight back against the unknown, and liked the indomitable nature that she was presenting. However, she was fighting the wrong person and now he hoped that he could heal her soon. That she was hurting and injured broke his heart. He was failing his Goddess given gift and he had not even been with her for a standard day. At least this kind of pain was temporary. He only worried that she would be incompatible to their healing parasites. He would find out soon as Kirrek and Sameth gave him the signal it was clear to morph.

Hailey whimpered with the pain in her foot, and tried to understand what was going on. Her foot should have connected with his sensitive parts. He should have dropped her to cover those parts and writhe on the floor in agony while she ran the other direction and escaped all of the aliens.

It should have been simple. She had even seen how all the events were going to play out inside her head, but then her foot connected and the agony Jarrek was supposed to feel became hers. He kept talking to her, but she was lost, floating in a sea of pain. It hurt so much she was nauseous.

Between one blink and the next, she found herself in a new place. The way these alien guys moved was disconcerting. She really was going to puke. Jarrek set her gently on a side seat and started calling out orders.

As soon as they completed the morph, Jarrek immediately called out for departure and for Kirrek and Sameth to join him. He leaned down and as gently as he could, he set his burden down, keeping her hand. He needed to ask her so many questions. He did not even know her name, but first he wanted her healed.

"I want to introduce you to my brother and cousin little bird. This is Kirrek and our cousin Sameth. Sameth is a wonderful healer and will look you over to see if he can relieve any of your pain." Jarrek said as he caressed the back of her hand. Turning to Sameth, he told him about his little birds attempt to flee and how she hurt her foot. Both men smiled at his words for a brief moment and clapped him on each shoulder, as a feisty woman was always a delight in bed.

Sameth knelt down to the tiny female, picking up her foot gently he probed the area and knew it was broken. He called out for his bag and once it was in hand, pulled out the hypo-dialer. The little female was so small he was scared to give her very much;

she was not much bigger than the pimba cats at home. He hoped that five units would help her until they got to the ship and he could determine her genetic make-up. Once he figured out if she was compatible with their medicine, he could get some healiogel into her break. "This won't hurt at all." Sameth told her as he gently gave her the pain relief. She was so beautiful. His Prince was a lucky man. That a mate had been found after all their eons searching was such a miracle. He allowed himself to hope that where one mate was, others would follow. Goddess willing, even one for him.

The one Jarrek called Sameth had the gentlest eyes she had ever seen. He was about two inches shorter than Jarrek's seven feet but while Jarrek and Kirrek where dark haired Sameth had long, flowing and beautiful blonde hair. He had the sides braided and held together in the back, while leaving the bottom free to lay over his shoulders. His gentle eyes were black and gold, but they shone with a light that made her feel as though she was with an angel. His Raphael-like good looks should have made her drool, but he just left her feeling as if she had fallen in love with a puppy. She had no understanding of exactly what he was saying, but this close she couldn't help but look directly into his eyes. She instinctively relaxed and let him help her. Within moments, the pain receded and she relaxed the tight grip she had on Jarrek's hand and took a deep breath.

"Why did you take me with you? Are you going to help me get home?" She asked Sameth. He didn't make her body sing and with those eyes, he was a little easier to approach.

Sameth looked from her to Jarrek and stood. He would leave conversation to her mate. Especially as his translator was still struggling with the language, she spoke. It appeared as though her language had many words that could mean a variety of different things. It was the context in which they came together that allowed the hearer to pick the right ones. It was quite exhausting. A couple of words he found he could not decipher the meaning. What exactly was barbequed? He would have to remember to ask her later when his translator and symbiot helped him learn her language. He moved away to see if any of his brothers had wounds to tend.

Jarrek was holding on to his symbiot by the thinnest of threads. His need to claim her was overwhelming and only the fact that she was injured had halted him from throwing her over his shoulder and finding some privacy. When his little bird relaxed the grip she had on his hand as her pain had lessened, his control almost slipped again. It was sheer determination that he not frighten her more than she already was that had allowed him to get a hold of his control a second time.

When she had asked Sameth if they were going to take her home, he had almost roared out his denial. She was his! His mate! His to care for, love, protect. Now that he had found her, he would collapse worlds to keep her. Only in death would he release her, and then only until she joined him. He had waited fourteen hundred and seven years for a mate. To lose her back on her world would drive him insane. He could never allow her to see her world again. She would forgive him one day, as he would make her so happy she forgot the little marble she came from. Tugging her hand to get her attention he said, "May I have your name first little bird?"

"My name is Hailey. Now answer my question."

"I am taking you to my home Hailey. You are my Cordisa, my heart's fate, and it will be my great joy to care for you. I know you have many questions. I also have many questions, but I ask you for patience on this. I would like to have Sameth complete your healing when we reach my ship. Afterward, we can discuss your situation and answer one another's questions. I will also have you fitted with a translator so that you can understand what the others are saying and learn my language as well."

"Great." Hailey thought to herself, from one situation to the next. The problem with this "situation" is that she had to fight her traitorous body. She wanted to stay with Jarrek. His nearness made her feel very horny, weirdly she also felt safe. She didn't believe in love at first sight or destined mates though. They were lines men handed out like crumbs to the starving.

They never meant them. Well, they did until they got what they wanted. Then, it was, "Hey, thanks for the ride." or even, "You're nice to fuck, but I can't be seen dating a fat chick." In her experience, men only gave you lines like that for their own agenda. They didn't even see the pain they caused.

For a very long time, she believed that someday she would find her prince charming and he would love her the way she was. However, too many times she met a man who wined and dined and made promises galore, but, after they got her into bed, it was goodbye.

Then she met Greg. For eight months they had dated and she had allowed herself to hope he was they one. He had proposed, she had said yes and he had moved in with her. After a month the comments started. "You know that food isn't good for you.

You should eat more salads. I don't understand why you can't just lose a little weight for me. If you loved me, you would try to look better. I'm not taking you out in public. Look at you; you aren't even trying to lose the pounds." Hailey had gotten so depressed she had contemplated suicide. Her mom had saved her. She had shown up at her apartment and dragged her out of bed.

"What are you doing, Hailey? You've changed, and not for the better. Where is your fire? Six months ago, you would have shown me Greg's nuts in a jar if he had humiliated you or gave you crap about your size and now you are bowing your head to this man and taking it. Why?"

"'Cuz there's no point mama. I am fat. I try to lose weight, but it just seems to stay there. I tried the bike, the pool, the elliptical machine and even the Zumba class. Men only want skinny women."

"Well then, that is their loss. You can only ever be yourself, Hailey. You are not responsible for how the rest of the world looks at you or feels. God made you just perfect, honey. You should never have to put up with someone who abuses you, and that is exactly what is happening here. Don't let him get away with it."

"I know you're right mama, but I get tired of being alone. I want to share my life with someone. I need someone to touch me."

"We all want to connect with somebody Hailey, but there is no reason you have to change to do so."

That conversation with her mom had started to put the fire back in her belly. She took less and less from Greg and finally packed his belongings and told him that he didn't live there anymore. She eventually moved closer to her mom and then they had bought a house together. It was the best decision she had ever made.

She had begun to heal, but now she found herself in a situation she could not have prepared for. She longed for Jarrek and deep down was in love with the idea of them being fated, but experience had taught her otherwise. She would just have to remind herself of all the lines a man could spin to get his way to help keep her grounded with reality, not fantasy.

Hailey pulled her hand from Jarrek and told him, "I am not your fate. I would like you to return me home now. I can take myself to the hospital there to get fixed up. You have no right… to…," She had only a brief warning before she could feel the darkness of sleep rush to her on speeding wings.

Jarrek quickly caught Hailey before she could slide off the seat and scooped her into his arms. He called for Sameth to make sure that she was not reacting poorly to their medicine. Once Sameth advised that she was just sleeping, he sat down with her cradled close to his chest and watched her sleep.

He could not wait to get her back to the destroyer where Sameth could take her to medical and heal her. Once that was complete and Sameth ran all the tests he needed to, Jarrek was going to take Hailey to his rooms and closet them both inside until he had sunk his cock in every part of

her body, worshiped every delectable inch
with his mouth, lips and tongue and made
her is bonded Cordisa. He was eager to be
her Prateo Corduva. Her heart fated, bonded
husband and protector.

3.

A Little Healing

Jarrek exited the shuttle carrying his Cordisa. Turning in the direction of the medical bay, he walked in long ground eating strides, not even taking the time to acknowledge any of his warriors who called out for orders or shouted questions.

He would speak to them after he had taken care of Hailey. She was and always would be his first consideration. Jarrek was quite sure that Kirrek could handle getting everything in order, and no doubt, his men would be spreading the wonderful and astonishing news that he had found his Cordisa.

Walking through the medical bay's doors, he strode to the nearest open station and with the greatest of care, laid the woman who now held his heart and soul down, straightening her limbs and making her more comfortable. Sameth was there next to him a few moments later, bringing Hailey's bag and an array of scanners, devices and blood collectors.

"If you could remove her foot coverings my Prince, I will begin running diagnostics on her overall anatomy and physiology. Once I get an idea of the composition inside, and how it functions on her species, the nannites will have collected bone, marrow and tissue samples. Then I can collect blood and hair samples. These first scans will also show me her reproducing capabilities." Sameth went around putting words into action.

"Once I have that information, I will know if I can inject the healiogel into her foot to knit the bone back together. These first scans will only take about fifteen minutes, I will need to run deeper and longer scans, but I will be using the information that I collect now so that you may take her to your rooms to finish recovering if that is your wish."

Jarrek looked up briefly from Hailey's face and said, "I would prefer it greatly. I treasure all of my people, but I have been granted a gift and do not want to share it with them just yet. Look at her Sameth," Jarrek said and went back to watching her beautiful face. Keeping it there, he continued. "I worry that I will harm her somehow. I know that the Goddess has made her specifically for me, but I am surprised by her size. How can something so small and fragile handle our way of life? Will she be able to take my passion for her? I will be as gentle as possible, but a warrior's lust can be all consuming on occasion. I have hurt Loku without meaning to and he is a warrior."

"My Prince, I do not mean you any disrespect, but I believe you are underestimating your female. She has shown us an incredibly indomitable spirit. Did she not manage to escape from her prison without our influence?" Sameth questioned. Remembering her ass, made him uncomfortably hard, so he moved around the table, surreptitiously adjusting his cock. He continued easing his cousin's mind with, "She is quite surprising. Yes, she is small, but I have no doubt that she would rise above any challenge victorious. Did she not break her foot trying to kick you in the balls? Any other species she encountered, she would have easily escaped. Our armor is deceptive and a secret we hold dear, it is the only reason she is hurt now. She is fierce and lovely. Small packages can often contain the indestructible items. Our teachings of the Goddess have taught us that. Have faith in her cousin." Sameth finished taking his samples and turned from Jarrek, lest he notice his still hard cock. He hoped it would go down soon or at least long enough for Jarrek to retire with Hailey. He really needed to go find relief.

Jarrek gave a small laugh and smiled at Sameth's words. "You speak truth Sameth. I see her size and fear; instead, I should realize her actions have spoken louder. I still will need to spank her ass for the dangerous stunt she pulled in her escape.

If she had fallen, all would have been lost and I would be a broken man. As soon as you are done, I will retire to my chambers and keep watch over her, while I find out just how far we are from being able to jump. If I remember correctly, we are still three weeks away from any known jump point. We must return to Athria as soon as possible. I will send a directive to all departments that I want every drop of power concentrated on getting us to the jump point as fast as possible. I cannot run the risk that she will be harmed. I will retire from killing the Krakill and spend my days loving Hailey and showing her my planet. "

Sameth put the last of his collection syringes away and said, "If you can give me about sixty microsecs I will be finished. I just need to inject the healiogel into her break and then we can put her foot covering back on and she is all yours."

Once Sameth finished the injection, they both helped put on her weird looking boots. Sameth would have liked to examine her strange garments, but would not bother his Commander and Prince with something so trivial at this time.

"There we are, she is ready to retire. She should sleep the rest of the night and maybe into the late afternoon tomorrow. I am afraid that even five units was more than her body is designed for. Now that I have some answers on some of her physiology, I will be prepared for any issues that may arise. I would like to be the first to offer my congratulations to your impending bond, my Prince, and say that I am very happy for you. That there is hope for our people at long last is a miracle." Sameth held out his arm so that he could clasp forearms with Jarrek.

Once Jarrek had accepted Sameth's felicitations, he picked up his intended bride and her bag and carried her to his rooms. Once she was ensconced on the bed, he wondered if he should remove any of her coverings. He had forgotten to ask Sameth if her species got cold at the temperature they kept the ship. Running his hand down her face, he found her to be a comfortable warm temperature, so decided to leave her as she was for now. He needed to send out his directives and have a meal. Then he could keep watch over his Cordisa while she healed.

4.

Kidnapped Again.

Hailey heard the sound of her alarm going off from a distance and wondered briefly, why it was so far away. She must have knocked it over again. Well it would go off again in five minutes. She just needed a few more minutes to try to catalog the weird dream she just had. Wow. She knew she had an active imagination, but damn. Stinky aliens she could probably figure out fairly easy as Bart slept in bed with her most days and he could stink up any room in five minutes once he started sleeping.

She loved the fat ball of fur, but it was as if he saved his gas all day just so that he could fart all night long in her bed. She had kicked him out of the bed more nights than she could count and once sent him to the greenhouse for a week because he had tangled with a skunk and came out the loser. She must have been sleeping hard not to have woken up and kicked him out. Hunky red aliens that could pop out of cages were a little tougher. The sexy part she got, but not why they were red.

Well, maybe it just meant that she was approaching a higher level of horniness and her little rabbit was not going to do the job this time around. Speaking of, maybe she could get in a quick orgasm. That Jarrek was panty melting. She was wishing she had jumped him in the dream so she had something to think back on when she reached down to play with her clit and encountered denim and not the elasticized cotton band of her pajamas.

"Huh?" She opened her eyes and looked down at herself. She was wearing the clothes from her dream. "Weird. Maybe I took a nap and had a very vivid dream." Turning her head, she expected to see her office bedroom, but instead stared into Jarrek's obsidian and silver eyes. "Son of a cow!" She shouted, scrambling to sit up and move away.

"Easy little bird. You are safe with me on my ship. No one here will ever hurt you. I would eviscerate them where they stood." Jarrek crooned in a soft voice to help soothe her.

"Holy Shit! Is that supposed to make me feel better? I thought everything was just a dream. Wait. I broke my foot on you. Why doesn't it hurt? Oh who cares, your real!" Hailey felt the tears come then. She tried to suck them back in, but it was useless. It was all real and she didn't know what would happen to her, or when she would get to see her mom again. It was all too much. To find herself kidnapped, not once, but twice? To aliens?

Dropping her head in her hands, she sobbed. "Oh God, Momma. What's gonna happen to me?" She felt Jarrek pick her up and croon to her, but she could not focus on his words and had no energy to fight him.

Jarrek saw the water start to pool in her beautiful eyes and quickly crossed the room to her. Scooping her into his arms, he lay back against the headboard and just held her as she cried. He felt so helpless in that moment. There was no one he could hurt to fix this, and for a while, as she adjusted to his world and life, she would experience these feelings many times.

All he could do holding her was to tell her repeatedly that he would, "swear upon all the stars in the sky, all of my ancestors throughout time itself, I will love, protect, and do everything in my power to make you happy." She held his heart and soul in her delicate hands. Once her sobs began to lessen, he stroked her hair and pressed kisses to it. She lifted her face to his; those red, water filled eyes seemed to scream to his soul to kiss her and remove her pain.

Looking up into his eyes, exhausted from crying, her pussy still grew moist as he bent his head towards her. She willingly met his kiss. Tired of fighting her body's response to him, Hailey had decided she would sate herself in his arms. Forever may not be possible, but right now was just fine. She wanted to know what his skin tasted like. To memorize the hills and ridges of his body, to feel the way he would cover her body and surround her in himself. To feel how his cock would stretch her pussy. She wanted to luxuriate in every delicious, inventive way that he would come up with to please her body. Hailey wanted to surrender to Jarrek and feel something other than the pain of her situation.

Hailey immediately opened her mouth to taste his lips. She began to lick and nibble as Jarrek did the same. Oh, the feel of his tongue against hers, he somehow tasted of dark orange chocolate. The dance of twining tongues together, of him tasting the recesses of her mouth left her feeling enraptured. She felt as though there was no part of her mouth left unexplored.

She pressed her body as tight against him as she could manage. Turning into him fully and straddling his legs, she rubbed her pussy against him, ramping her desire for him higher, and she was sure leaving a wet stain on his crotch. The hard, thick length of his cock teased her clit and had her panting and trying to rip the clothes from his body.

He felt so huge, so good. She needed to feel his skin. "Strip. Hurry. I need skin, oh, that feels so good." She cried as he pushed his rigid cock up against her, digging her denim harder against her clit. It added pressure and increased the pleasure. "Skin, give me naked skin." She chanted at him while trying to help him remove his clothes, and sucking on his neck, ear, even the line of his jaw.

Jarrek felt as though he had died and gone to be with the Goddess. Hailey eating at his lips, twining their tongues together was so delicious he felt as though he could sip at them for hours. He explored her mouth as though it held the secrets to the universe. His cock filled and throbbed. He pushed up against her to help relieve some of the agony in his cock. He would need to remove his armor soon or it would kill him. She seemed to read his mind, pulling at his armor and telling him to remove it. Pulling his lips from her only caused her to attack his neck, his ears. A little shiver ran through him as she found a spot just under his ear that made his arousal grow.

He scrambled to find the buttons under the band of his pants that would open the seams on his armor. Quickly pushing all of them, he tore apart his armor from shoulder to waist. Dragging them down each arm, he flung each piece to the side of the bed and wrapped his arms around his lush Cordisa once more. He leaned her back and laid her out across the mattress. As she ran her small hands all over his chest and flanks, he tried to find the tabs to remove her clothing.

Frustrated and wanting her skin against his, he leaned up, grabbed a handful of her material and ripped it from her body. They both froze. Jarrek froze because the beauty of her skin and her abundant breasts in their black lace covering held him in awe. Hailey froze from insecurity due to past relations. She was just starting to think that maybe this was a bad idea when the breath just seemed to leave his body on a loud groan saying, "Goddess incarnate."

Jarrek wanted this first time they were together to be etched and burned into his memory for all time. He tried to tell her how he felt. "You are so beautiful I cannot think of a way to let you know just how perfect you really are, except to say that you are one of the Goddesses reborn into flesh. I want to look at all of you, how can I remove the covering?" he asked pointing to her bra.

With trembling hands, Hailey reached behind her and said, "Let me." Unhooking her bra, she slowly peeled it off, teasing him a little by using on arm to cover her breast while she tossed her bra to the side. Jarrek was having none of it. Pushing her arms down, he let his eyes devour her. Watching as her nipples grew distended and tight.

He covered her body with his, straddling one leg. He pushed his thigh high against her pussy and bending, he captured a peak in his mouth. He sucked, sipped, and bit her flesh. He squeezed and teased her other nipple, plucking and giving it rough twists on occasion. She made the most beautiful noises under him as she clutched and pulled his hair. Pushing her cunt up and grinding it against his thigh, Jarrek was ready to hear her cries of completion. He switched his attention to her other breast, and pushed his thigh higher against her pussy. Taking her nipple between his teeth, he bit down on the tip and then sucked her tit deep in his mouth. He felt her nails dig deep into his head and her high keening cry of completion as she continued to grind against him and he luxuriated in the sounds and scent of his Cordisa's release.

Ready to finish striping them both bare so that he could sink his cock deep inside her sheath and start the bonding ceremony, Jarrek let out several curses and a moan of denial when a loud ring came from his bedside. Rolling off his sated Cordisa was one of the hardest things Jarrek had done in a very long time. Grabbing up his link, he depressed the connection and shouted "What?" into it.

"I am sorry Commander, but you are needed on the bridge. We have Krakill's pursuing us, and you are going to want to see this." Loku replied in a bland tone.

"Loku, this better be very important. They are Krakill's. You should be able to handle this." Jarrek replied.

"Yes Commander. I agree. I am still saying that you are going to want to see this." Loku replied in the same monotone.

"On my way. And Loku, I suggest you start praying to the Goddess I don't kill you when I get there." Jarrek ended the call and started putting his armor back on. His cock was going to be black and blue from his armor's stranglehold.

Turning to Hailey to apologize for the interruption and to let her know that he had to return to the bridge, he was surprised to find her asleep again. Returning her back to her original position in the bed, he covered her up and kissed her cheek. He strode out of his room contemplating if he should kill Loku, confident he would return before she awoke.

5.

<u>*A Real Cordisa?*</u>

Kirrek, finally finished with his duties from this latest mission, exited the lift and quickly walked towards the engineering offices. The expression on his face was so fierce it caused crewmembers to remove themselves from the path. Whatever his destination, they were very glad that he was not set on them. They sent a quick prayer to the Goddess for the poor bastard he was after. If the person were lucky, he would not feel much before he met Her. Slamming into a general break room, he caused all conversation to stop. "Out!" He roared. Cups of coffee and late evening meals left behind, as all of the occupants made haste to exit. Kirrek did not watch their departure, did not even see them any longer. He had found his quarry shortly after slamming through the door. He pinned him with his stare and stalked towards him. The door had barely shut when he reached Sidhawk and grabbed him by the back of the neck.

"I am sorry Sidhawk, but this will probably not be pleasant for you." He quickly pushed Sidhawk to his knees gripping his neck in a bruising hold with one hand, while freeing his shaft from his trousers with the other.

"The Prince has found a Cordisa and she is lush and all you could want to find. I am in great need and require you to relieve me. Suck it. Take it all." Kirrek aimed his straining shaft at Sidhawk's lips and pushed forward. Grabbing both sides of Sidhawk's head, he tightened his grip on his shoulder length black hair and fucked his mouth is long, hard jabs. Sidhawk gagged a little at the quickness of his strokes before finally relaxing his throat.

"Tighten your lips on me." He demanded of Sidhawk.

"Oh, yes. Just like that. I love when you swallow my cock like that. Suck me all down." Closing his eyes, Kirrek thought back to that lush ass climbing down those bars. Within moments, he was shouting his release. Letting his grip on Sidhawk lessen, he helped pull him to his feet.

"Remove your clothing. I am not done with you yet, are you still loose from last joining or do you need me to loosen you up?" Kirrek questioned, but spoke again before Sidhawk could answer. "No matter. Hurry, I will go a little easier now that you have taken the edge off."

Kirrek impatiently helped him strip and then bent him over the table. "Goddess, Sidhawk. Wait until you see her. All long hair and lush, round beauty."

With his cock still rock hard and gleaming with spit from fucking Sidhawk's mouth and his own seed, he pushed his shaft inch by inch into his tight hole.

"Oh yes, Sidhawk. Grip me with your tight ass. I will make it up to you, love. Later I will let you top me for a change."

Once he had bottomed out, he set up a smooth, hard pace. He hoped that he was going a little easier on Sidhawk as he would need to fuck him many times to lose this hunger. Kirrek began fucking him harder and continued.

"I will take you to see my brother's Cordisa in a little while and you will see why I needed you so much. I didn't hurt you, did I?"

"No Kirrek. I can take your passion. I welcome it." Sidhawk answered with a voice gravelly from Kirrek's rough treatment and pushed back against his lover. "Take me. Fuck my ass. Describe this beauty to me."

"She is small in stature. She only comes up to the bottom of Jarrek's breast plate, but she has ripe, full globes for breasts, which make you want to sip of their bounty for hours. Just imagining what they would look like full of milk as she feeds a child has me amped up, and wanting to find one for myself." He picked up his pace. Sidhawk's tight, warm ass coupled with what he was describing had him losing control again. He widened his legs and angled up on each thrust to make sure that he caught Sidhawk's pleasure spot. When he heard Sidhawk's breathless moans reach the right pitch, he continued his description.

"Her breasts would overflow my hands they are so ripe. She has this ass. Oh Goddess, her ass is perfection. Like yours all full, plump and just made to cushion a man's hard thrusts." Giving Sidhawk several deep thrusts to as he said it.

"Oh yeah, keep squeezing my cock. I am close." Kirrek praised Sidhawk. With one hand clutching his shoulder to help power into his strokes, he reached under Sidhawk and squeezed his shaft hard. Sidhawk's groan of denial echoed up to him.

"Do not release yet my Sidhawk. I will reward your patience. Take me. Take my essence now." With a last hard thrust, Kirrek pushed deep inside his ass and let loose his own pleasure, groaning loudly in the empty room. A few gentle thrusts, to milk his shaft dry and Kirrek gently pulled out and turned Sidhawk around. Bending over he sucked Sidhawk's shaft deep into his throat, released his tight grip on Sidhawk's shaft and quickly brought him screaming over the edge.

After they had caught their breath and redressed, Kirrek again made sure that Sidhawk was okay. He had taken him hard this time. While not the first time he had lost control, it was however; the most violent he had been in decades. Sidhawk usually left Kirrek feeling quite protective of him and conscious of his size. At barely six feet, Sidhawk stood at the low end of the scale in size. His size was perfect for his position in engineering. Able to fit in spots others could not get to with their bulk and height. His voice was a little higher than most and he was quite lean, but had a round comfortable ass. His shoulder length, black hair with the little peak on his oval face, left him with a very delicate and feminine look. Beautiful copper and silver eyes that tilted up at the corners, thin arched brows, a pert little nose and lips that made a man want to sink his cock between them rounded out the very sweet picture of Sidhawk.

With the amount of lust in his system, even though he had come twice so quickly, Kirrek was struggling to keep those protective feelings in the forefront of his mind. With most of the population men, they had turned to their own sex for relief. Yes, there were pleasure houses on Athria, but they could only handle so many patrons in a day and were quite expensive. Moreover, most of their missions took them into space, killing the Krakill's and looking for a compatible species to breed with; it was not conducive for women to be aboard a fighting ship. As females were treasured, they could not take the risk of them coming to harm in battle. Hundreds of mechanized, female sex-bots were included in the supplies of every ship, but most craved warm flesh to surround their cocks. Doctors had deemed that giving relief to one another as healthy. Occasionally a strong love bond formed, allowing them to be monogamous with each other. So, that while not Corduva, or fated hearts, some considered them in the same category and respected their bond. Kirrek had been with Sidhawk for almost a thousand years and such a bond had formed early in their relationship.

"Let us get back to our quarters. We both need a shower and I need you again." Leading Sidhawk out of the room, he told him, "I bet all the team that went on this last mission is busy doing the same thing I just did to you. Once you take off my edge again, I promise to take you to meet her. She should have a translator by now."

Sidhawk stopped abruptly and asked Kirrek with incredulity in his voice. "Wait. You mean that Jarrek has actually found a Cordisa? This is not some sexual game you are playing with me?"

"No love. Varill had already kidnapped this female from the small blue and white planet before we arrived on his ship. He and his crew somehow managed to capture all of us. Now, no one knows why he did not just kill us all and continue on his mission, whatever that entails, but he did not. The female had managed to cut through many of the bars on her cell and she climbed down from the cage to the floor by herself. Her ass was on display for all of us to lust over. Once we all quit trying to yell at her to not climb out of the cage, that we would come get her, we all held our breath hoping this little female would not fall to her death, or get hurt. I think we all were poised to morph to her at the first hint she was going to fall. Even if it meant having to be stuck behind while our symbiot recharged. All of us would have risked capture and death so that she and Jarrek would survive. Do you see the implications of this? The Goddess has seen fit to save us."

"Blessed Goddess." Sidhawk praised. "I never thought I would see the day. A Cordisa. Kirrek take me to meet her now please. I think I have to see this with my own eyes." Sidhawk pleaded.

"Looking all disheveled and smelling of sex?" Kirrek teased his normally fastidious partner.

"Yes Kirrek. I do not think I can wait." Sidhawk stated with complete sincerity. He had to see this miracle for himself. To find a female capable of mating with them? Carrying their child? No, he had to see this sight for himself with no delay.

"All right, love. Let's go." Kirrek turned them to the bank of elevators. He hoped Jarrek was not busy with the little female. If they interrupted something intimate, they would not survive long. Kirrek was quite surprised when they ran into Jarrek just outside the elevator. "Jarrek? What is wrong?"

"I have been called to come to the bridge. Loku says that I must see something that the Krakill's are doing, since they are following us. I am still deciding if I should kill him or not." Jarrek replied matter of fact.

"What? Why? Loku is your best friend and completely loyal." Kirrek was astonished to hear Jarrek say that he was deciding if he should kill Loku in that tone. Jarrek and Loku had shared many nights together, much like he and Sidhawk. It would be like hearing those words come from his mouth. Inconceivable.

"I was with Hailey." Jarrek said shortly. Letting the tone of his voice clearly imply what he would not speak aloud.

Clearing his throat Kirrek replied, "Of course. Understandable. I was wondering if I could introduce Sidhawk to your Cordisa then. They could entertain one another while you are otherwise engaged."

"She is asleep again. I will allow him to watch over Hailey until my return, while you come with me. If I have to kill Loku I will need you to watch the bridge." Jarrek joked deadpan.

"Of course, brother. I will let Sidhawk into your rooms and will meet you on the bridge." Kirrek replied. He knew as well as Jarrek, that Loku was in no danger of losing his life by Jarrek's hand. Continuing down the corridor, he led Sidhawk to his brother's rooms and keyed in his code. "I will return shortly." Kirrek said as he watched Sidhawk hurry into his brother's room.

Sidhawk quickly walked through the door, eager to see what this female looked like. He didn't' even look at Kirrek as he said goodbye and went to look at the female. Hailey was such a strange name. He wondered what it meant. Finally seeing what Kirrek was talking about made Sidhawk's jaw drop open. If her name meant lushly beautiful, then he would believe it. Great Goddess above! She was a breath stealing vision for sure. Her curves were exactly right to hold a man. Kirrek had not done her justice. He would not be surprised to find she was a Goddess in flesh.

6.

A Disturbing Message

Jarrek strode onto the bridge with frustrated strides. Loku and he had been friends since birth. He could not remember a time in his life he had been without Loku's companionship, but right now, he would like to throw him out the nearest airlock. "Report!" He shouted after he had gotten two steps into the room, making his way to his chair.

Loku Rai Trindon strode to Jarrek's side saying, "It is not good Commander. Varill's ship is pursuing us vigorously, but that is not what I called you to witness. I would not have disturbed you for anything, as the ship was buzzing about the woman you carried to medical within two microsecs after your emergence from the shuttle. Who she is to you and the implications of your discovery has affected everyone aboard this ship. The news has even gone via fast capsule to Athria and your father. However, Varill has sent a message for you that I knew you would want to see."

"Then play his message." Jarrek demanded.

"You may wish to brace yourself Commander, it is very disturbing to see and," Loku began, before Jarrek waved his explanation away.

"I am not ignorant Loku. Frustrated as you interrupted the start of something wonderful, but never ignorant. I know that you would never interrupt me for something trivial. The bland tone you used on the link gave me the information that it will be quite horrific. Just get on with it."

"Yes, Commander. Play message." Loku ordered.

Varill's ugly countenance appeared on the large screen in front of him. He had a horrific parody of a smile on his face, lending him even more menace.

"My old friend Jarrek, why did you leave so soon? Well, it is always a pleasure to see you no matter how long you stay, but we had not quite reached the fun parts. I did not even get to give you any new scars. Such a shame, as you are not quite as pretty as I would like to make you. Not nearly as lovely as the prize you stole from me. I want my pet back Jarrek." Varill snarled, finally losing that fake smile.

"Go find your own pussy, friend. I was quite enjoying mine. Would you like to see? Hmm, I bet you would. Yes, show my friend Jarrek some of the wonderful things I got to enjoy with my pet before he so rudely stole her away."

His face vanished, only to be replaced by a nightmare. His Cordisa was unconscious, naked and restrained to a metal table. Varill was running his nasty claws all over her body. He watched them take their tests on her. Watched as Varill touched her sweet pussy and shoved his collection devices inside her, in a violent imitation of the sex act. Raping her delectable body, a body he had barely begun to worship. His poor love. He watched as day after day they stuck their collections devices inside her. Sometimes, several of the Krakill touched his precious little bird's body, sticking tubes down her throat, her belly, her ass and vagina.

Jarrek felt his blood boiling inside his veins, felt the tight reign he had on his emotions disintegrate and heard as his chair arms ripped from their foundation, almost throwing him on the floor. He let them go and regained his balance in his chair. The nightmare grew though as Varill came back to the screen.

"My little pet just seems to make nothing but eggs. Several of my men and I have been able to successfully use her ova and now incubate our young. I also hold in my possession one of yours." Varill showed a small egg, floating a pinkish liquid, in a rubbery looking balloon.

"After you took my little pet away, I was quite angry and threw a bit of a tantrum. Shameful, I know. Well, after killing several of my crew for allowing you to escape, I calmed down and tried to figure out why you had taken her with you. Normally, we play your boring game of, how many can I kill? This time, you snatched my pet and left in a hurry. Why? Well, I tried a little experiment. I took some of your frozen seed, reanimated it and introduced it to one of my pet's eggs. Would you like to know the results my little experiment meted? I will tell you. Your seed practically leapt to her eggs they vibrated so fast. I have never seen a species so fertile in all my searching. The little egg I showed to you, it is your daughter." Varill paused here for a moment, then started laughing very hard, but cut it off abruptly.

Jarrek leaned forward a little more, a growl already rumbling deep in his chest as he watched Varill.

"Well that was pleasant. Not what I commed you for though. I want my pet back Jarrek. I am even willing to trade her for your daughter. Well, it could be your daughter. Right now, it would be so easy to dispose of her. The first girl child conceived in, how long again? Six, seven, eight thousand years or so, hmm? If you refuse my very generous offer, I may let your daughter live just long enough to see if we can harvest eggs from her, with the introduction of such a fertile species, who knows what the results would be? You have three days to make up your mind. After that we will be blow up your ship. I cannot risk going too far from this fertile planet. I look forward to your answer."

With that, the screen went blank and Jarrek was glad he was still sitting down. His mind was going a thousand directions at once and did not know what to latch on to first. His Cordisa's torture and rape, that she was so fertile to both of their species, or that she had young on board that ship? How about the surprising news that Varill still had some of his genetic material, or that he was going to be a father. A father to a female child, no less than his entire population's hope.

He looked at Loku and then to Kirrek, whose entrance he had missed during that horrific message. For one terrible moment, he wondered if he would be up to this task. He felt fragile in a way he never had before. Then it all fast-forwarded and punched him right in the solar plexus. Breathless and reeling, it still managed to straighten his spine and harden his resolve.

Varill needed to die right now. Not later, not after he made sure his whole planet protected his Cordisa, but before they ran out of time to answer Varill's message. "He dies now!" Jarrek shouted and threw back his head and issued a war cry that did not need a speaker to carry it throughout the ship. It sped and vibrated, touching his people on board and resonating within their hearts.

"Kirrek, Loku I want plans and contingency plans drawn up. I want a bomb expert in here to speak with me in two hours. I must speak with my Cordisa about what has happened. I will want her help to make some decisions about her young. Send another message to my Father letting him know what has occurred. I also want a signal sent out to the other destroyers. I want as many as possible to make their way to me and mine at once. I will return as soon as possible. Make ready."

"Yes Commander." They both saluted and turned away to begin making plans. They were both reeling from the messages contents. Loku had heard part of the beginning of the message, but not all and his blood lust fired up to an all-time high. This cat and mouse game with Varill had gone on too long. It was time for them to get serious and take them out. He closed his eyes and said a quick prayer to the Goddess of all Life to watch over Jarrek's precious daughter and Cordisa. He would need her strength for the coming battle he was sure.

Kirrek felt as though someone had blind-sided him. He had walked onto the bridge right as Varill's face turned into the torture of Jarrek's Hailey. Those images now carved into his memory for all time. He could not imagine the pain his brother must be feeling. It is one thing to hear what atrocities had happened to his Cordisa, but to have seen them taking place along with the rest of his men, it must be a special kind of hell.

To have the knowledge that the same savages that had hurt and tortured his love had his daughter? May the Goddess help him! The universe was about to burn in the heat of Jarrek's wrath. Varill could not understand what kind of animal he just unleashed.

Well, he would be dead before he could contemplate it fully. He felt honored to help Jarrek plan this battle. His niece's life and the life of his planet counted on their victory and he would not let any of them down.

7.

A Small Explanation

Hailey could feel the smile on her face as she floated up from sleep. The orgasm Jarrek had given her had taken everything out of her. Now she was ready to start again and finally feel him sink into her body. She shivered in delight at the thought and reached for Jarrek as she turned over. Her hand touched cold sheets. Where was Jarrek? Surely, he had stuck around to hold her as she slept. I mean he hadn't gotten off yet. That tended to leave a man desperate enough to do the cuddle thing. "Jarrek?" She called out.

"I'm afraid he had to go to the bridge. I was tasked with your well-being until his return." A voice said from the shadow next to the door. "My name is Sidhawk. I am lover to Kirrek, whom I believe you have met."

Hailey whipped her head in that direction and pulled the sheet closer to her body, making sure she was covered.

"Um, yeah. Jarrek's brother I think. Or cousin? No, that was Sameth. They are the only two I have met so far. I'm Hailey. So you're Kirrek's lover? That's cool. I didn't think when I met an alien they would turn out to be gay. Well, I didn't even think that people from other planets were real, you know? So how could they be gay or straight? Sorry. I'm nervous. I tend to ramble when I'm nervous."

Sidhawk came closer to Hailey and smiled down on her. "I am unsure what gay or straight mean to you. Could you please elaborate on this for me?"

"Oh, sure. Do you think I could get a shirt or something to cover up with first? I'm not used to having' a conversation without clothes on." Hailey asked.

"Well if you must, but you are quite stimulating to look at and I am quite enjoying the way you look right now. Your lovely hair all tangled and messy, your sexy shoulders bare. I really love the little hint of your nipples poking against the sheet. You are the most beautiful woman I have seen in a very long time. At least, a living one. We have a lovely statue of the Goddess in the chapel on board where we go to pray. I will show you one day." Sidhawk replied.

"Thanks, I think. Now I'm confused. I could have sworn that you said you were Kirrek's lover. On my planet, we have men and women who aren't attracted to the opposite sex, but the same sex as they are. Women who fall in love and have sex with other women and men who fall in love, and have sex with other men. This term is gay. I thought you only found other men attractive. Am I wrong on that?" Hailey explained.

"Well not wrong. Let me tell you a little bit about our planet Athria. This will explain it for you I believe. We are actually a dying race of men, my dear. There are only five thousand women or less left alive on my entire world. Not one of those women is under the age of six thousand." Sidhawk began as he pulled the chair closer to the bedside and sat down.

"Whoa. Stop right there. How old?" Hailey stopped Sidhawk; certain she had heard that wrong. There was no way he had said thousand.

"That we have had no females for about six thousand years or that there are females on my planet over six thousand years old?" Sidhawk queried.

"That the women on your world are over six thousand years old? How is that possible? I am twenty-six years old. The people on my planet can live to about one hundred years old. Some can live a little longer, but not more than one hundred and twenty-five. I mean wow! Wait. How old are you? You look about my age." Hailey hoped that Sidhawk didn't take offense to her question, but she was incredibly curious. So caught up in the fascinating conversation that she didn't realize she still was naked from the waist up and only the sheet covered her from his gaze.

"I am one thousand two hundred and fifteen. Jarrek is about fourteen hundred and fifty. Kirrek is eight years older than I am. We have a symbiotic relationship with a parasite on our planet that helps to extend our lives and gives us other amazing attributes, like morphing. I will explain that in more detail later if you like. But for now can I finish explaining about gay and straight?" Sidhawk patiently answered.

"Oh, I'm sorry. Of course. You just blew my mind away with the age thing. You keep explaining and I will pay attention." Hailey apologized.

Sidhawk crossed his leg and began where he left off. "Only Jarrek and Kirrek's mother was born after that. Unfortunately, she was lost to us eleven hundred years ago when she died after complications from childbirth. She gave birth to Jarrek and Kirrek's stillborn brother Marrek then hemorrhaged. There was so much damage; even her symbiot could not help heal her. It was a sad day for our planet for many reasons. She was the last female born on our planet, and she was extremely fertile, having three pregnancies within a three hundred year span. We had hoped she would give birth to a girl child. We already knew we were dying, but even one woman lost is a devastating blow to us all." Sidhawk paused and bowed his head for a brief moment in honor of Laria passing.

Clearing his throat, Sidhawk resumed, but pulled out a small tablet. "We have been searching the universe for a species that could be compatible with us reproductively for about four thousand years. Jarrek's grandfather started sending out large destroyer ships full of scientist and warriors to search every planet and moon they came across for a species that could help breathe life into our dying race. In the meantime, we needed relief. Of course, other species out in the universe while not compatible to reproduce with could still provide relief to our males. We have many pleasure houses all over our planet and pay them very well indeed. Unfortunately, they are expensive to most soldiers and there are only so many they can accommodate in a day. Even working thirty-three hours a day on a rotation cannot accommodate all our warriors. We are legion and they are few. Thus, we turned to our fellow warriors for relief. Now Kirrek and I share a love bond and have for the last thousand years, but not every warrior falls in love with the people chosen to relieve themselves. It is healthy to help relieve a brother warrior. It keeps the aggression down on ships like this where there is nothing to work out the energy. There is no need for them to form stronger bonds unless they want them. Does this help to clarify my term for you?" Sidhawk asked as he finished replicating several changes of clothing for Hailey on his tablet. A small chime sounded to the left of the bed and Sidhawk stood and crossed the wall. Pushing on a flashing strip of light a drawer opened and Sidhawk removed a piece of material.

"Here take this and go change. When you are through, you can ask me as many questions as you like. I will answer as best as I can." He told her handing her a new dress. Wrapping the sheet around her, she went off to the side room and quickly changed clothes. Figuring out the toilet and the water to wash her hands took so long; she finally just called Sidhawk in and let him explain how everything worked. She wanted to figure it out on her own, but didn't want to push a button and have something try to eat her or suck her into space.

Hailey figured that was how her luck was running and she didn't need to tempt fate any further. She loved the dress. It reminded her of a Grecian design. Long, pale green, silky fabric gathered under her breast and around her waist to wrap around her body and tie under her breasts, the rest falling all the way to the bottoms of her feet. The top half tied behind her neck and at each shoulder, elbow and wrist, leaving a small gap that showed skin. It was so beautiful she couldn't help but twirl and pet the smooth fabric. "Thanks Sidhawk. This is the most beautiful gown I've ever worn."

Hailey told him when she returned to the room.

"That is nothing Hailey. I can't wait to see how you will be dressed when we can get you to my planet and Jarrek brings in the seamstresses'. That man will lavish all kinds of silks and jewels on you."

That statement quickly brought Hailey to her senses. "I don't think so. I want to go home to my planet. I've already told him I am not his Cordisa or whatever it is he called me and that I expect him to bring me back home."

"Why would you wish to go home when Jarrek will worship at your feet? My entire planet will rise up in your defense. You are my future Queen. When Jarrek's father passes to the next life, he will become King of Athria. As his Cordisa, you are literally fated to rule not only his heart, but also his planet. How can you not want to be loved like that?" Sidhawk asked her in genuine confusion. She was fated to be Jarrek's heart and soul. He could not conceive of someone not wanting that.

"Look Sidhawk, I know you don't understand. It's just I don't believe in fated mates or loving someone upon first sight. That is a fantasy and not something that I want to base a relationship on. Plus, why would he want me? I am fat and round. On my planet men, want women who are thin, tanned, and even toned with muscles. Round, over-weight women like me are nobodies and overlooked. There's no way I would be able to keep Jarrek interested in me. He'll find some other woman to share his life with."

"You could not be more wrong my dear. Every warrior on this ship would kill to worship at your feet. When Kirrek returned from Varill's ship, he stalked into the break room that I was in and threw everyone out. He forced me to my knees and took me with a force he had not used in a very long while. That is how turned on he was. The men on your planet must be idiots not to want to drop to their knees in worship of you. My body finds you very attractive. I know you are not my mate, but I still yearn for you. You are sexy, delicious and very desirable. I do not –", Sidhawk stopped abruptly and closed his eyes for several moments.

"Something is wrong." Sidhawk told Hailey. "Jarrek just sent out a war cry. Let me contact the bridge and find out what is going on." Sidhawk started towards the bedside comm, but turned to the door as it opened. He was prepared to defend Hailey to the death, but only Jarrek came striding in.

8.

It's Been How Long?

"Commander, is everything all right?" Sidhawk asked anxiously.

"Engineer First Class Barion. Please step outside so that I may speak with my Cordisa privately. If your duties are not pressing you may stay and guard Hailey." Jarrek commanded.

"If you have need of me, then of course I will stay. I would be honored to guard your Cordisa." Sidhawk replied and gave a little bow in Hailey's direction before stepping out of the room into the hall.

"Jarrek. What's wrong?" Hailey asked.

Jarrek strode to Hailey and took both of her hands in his. Leading her to the table by the prep station, he seated her and went down on one knee. Looking her in the eyes with a tortured expression Jarrek told Hailey everything he had just seen and the horrible bomb Varill had dumped in his lap.

"I don't think that can be right Jarrek. I mean, I was kidnapped only this morning, or maybe yesterday depending on how long I was out after Sameth gave me the shot. Are you sure?" Hailey began to think that maybe she was missing something, as this sounded a little far-fetched.

"Hailey I know for sure that Varill had been over your planet for the last week. We watched for several days making plans to sneak aboard and kill the crew, and speculating on what could interest him in the little planet. We did our own search and realized that it was the only planet to hold any kind of life forms. We began to get worried they had found the protein enzyme they were looking for and would call in reinforcements. It was why we decided to launch our attack right away. We could have stolen the ship, taken it to a different quadrant of space and let them think Varill's ship had been mistaken. When we found you, we left immediately. You have slept for the last twelve hours. The message that Varill sent also had video feeds of what they did to you. I can allow you to view the message if you think that you can handle the images. Otherwise, I must forbid you seeing them and just ask you what you would have me do with the eggs they fertilized with your ova. They are partly your children and I do not want to destroy them without knowing how you feel about it." Jarrek explained to her solemnly.

Hailey leaned close enough to Jarrek that their noses almost touched while she yelled at him and said, "Let me? Did you just say you would let me? Jarrek I want you to listen to me very carefully. If you ever attempt to hold me back or tell me what I can or can't do like some recalcitrant child you are about to discipline, I will find out if you have any balls and cut them right the fuck off. I am a grown ass woman and you will never dictate to me. Am I making myself very clear to you?" Hailey waited for Jarrek to blink at her before she leaned back in her seat and continued with, " I can see that you are trying and at least made an effort to tell me what is going on, but don't ever tell me what you decided to do on my behalf. My own father wouldn't have done that once I reached my majority. You don't have the right, not even if you were my heart's mate or fate. Not that I am saying we are, as you know I don't believe that we are fated to be together. I mean please! Now show me the message so that I can make some decisions."

Jarrek tried to understand why she was yelling at him. He was her Corduva and therefore responsible for her well-being. Part of his job was to make sure that she did not just go and make crazy decisions based on emotion and not logic. Females were prone to feel instead of think. Every man in the universe knew this to be true. Females had died because they acted on emotions instead of thinking.

"Little bird, if you believe us to be mated or no, it does not change the fact, that you are my Cordisa. It is my great joy and responsibility to love and protect you. Part of that protection includes making sure that you do not act on emotion instead of logic. I do not wish for you to have to see your own body raped. I did not enjoy seeing the images and could not imagine that you will either. This is my call, little bird and I am sorry if that upsets you."

Hailey pinched the bridge of her nose and bit down on her tongue. She wasn't going to fight Jarrek on this. She would go home and whatever responsibility he felt could go to the next female he met. She ignored the twinge in her heart that thought caused and sighed.

"Can you just play the message please Jarrek? I will need time to think about this and we don't have the time to delay."

"Of course, little bird. If you need a moment at any time just say pause message." Jarrek said as he stood and pressed in his access code to have the message replay. He returned to Hailey's side in case she needed his support.

Hailey watched the message and only had to pause it once, when her stomach tried to rebel from the images of her being violated. She was glad that her stomach was empty. Instead, she just dry heaved over the sink in the prep area. Jarrek brought her a cold glass of water and a damp towel. Once she had felt settled, she resumed the message.

When Varill showed her the image of the little bean like egg floating in what looked like amniotic fluid, she shivered and felt sick again. Once she felt she could open her mouth safely she told Jarrek, "Not even going to lie and say that was smooth. That was rougher than any bull at the rodeo back home, but I still think it has to be a lie. I don't usually blurt what I'm about to tell you to just anyone, but I can't have kids. I am RH negative so that needs a special shot, but I have a lot of scaring on my ovaries. The doctors have told me that the chances of my getting pregnant are almost a statistical impossibility. I produce many eggs, but they aren't viable. They just circle my ovaries, harden, and become cysts. The scarring is from many of the cysts growing so large they burst open. I want to believe I could be a mother, but I am hesitant to do so. Can you understand that?" Hailey almost pleaded with Jarrek.

Jarrek cupped Hailey's beautiful face in his hands and tried to convey the depths of his feelings for her while helping her to cope with what he knew to be true.

"I understand that you have a problem getting pregnant on your planet, but as I have told you before, you are my Cordisa. Your body was intended to be mine. You were intended to have my children. Perhaps this RH you speak of is just an indication that you are compatible with my species and not your own. The Goddess of All Life has created you specifically for me. I am telling you that this is true. This monster is holding our daughter. The only female child of my people conceived for the last six thousand years. I must attempt to rescue her and kill Varill and his entire ship. What I am asking you little bird, is do you wish me to kill the eggs that Varill and his crew have stolen and fertilized with their genetic material? Do you wish me to save them and try to bring them to you? This is all I would need to know, little bird." Jarrek brushed away the tears that rolled down her cheeks with his thumbs.

"I am so sorry my love. I promise I will kill Varill and as many Krakill as I can to avenge you."

The tears wouldn't stop coming. Hailey's heart was breaking and she had never wanted the advice of her momma so much before. "Jarrek, I am very confused about what to do. I want to save the eggs, but I wouldn't know what to do with them and I don't know if I could care for so many children at one time. Plus, I don't have the first clue how to keep them alive inside there, or what they would need when they hatched."

Hailey took a deep breath and swiped angrily at the tears on her face. "One thing I do know is that you need to snap, crackle and pop Varill and the others. Rice crispy all their asses. I would like to see Varill's head on a fucking platter and I don't mean the one on his ugly neck either!" Maybe the anger would help her, maybe not. Right now, in this instance, she felt could make no choice that would be the right one. "I need to think about the eggs for a bit, before I decide. I just keep seesawing' back and forth and I'm going to make myself dizzy if I don't move on and do something else."

Standing up, she wrapped her arms around her middle. "I think I need a bath to help relax me, but I also want to have you get some bleach so I can scrub my entire body raw. I don't like that they did all that to me and I don't even remember it. I honestly thought that it had just happened. Ugh, every thought I have is going back and forth. Does your bathroom, have something that I could fill with hot water?" Hailey question Jarrek.

Pulling her into his arms, he tightened his hold until she stilled. He wondered if she was aware that she was pacing back and forth and alternating between holding her middle and scrubbing at her arms. "I can take you into the cleanser. It does not have the ability to hold water for you to soak in, but it has rays of energy that burn off old skin and dirt until you are completely clean. We can do that if you like, but I don't think that is all you need." Jarrek told her as he started leading her to the cleansing room. "I can help you relax little bird and take your mind away from all this for just a few moments. Would you like that?"

"I would like to try to forget for a moment. I need to plan, and collect myself, but we don't have the time Jarrek. I need to come to some kind of decision. I will see if Sameth can remove all of my skin later. Sorry, sick bastard. I would like to barbeque his ass." Hailey muttered, pulling herself from Jarrek's arms and continuing to pace.

"One day we are going to have time to sit down so you can explain this barbeque to me. Right now, I want you to come here." Jarrek told Hailey, pulling her attention back to him where it belonged.

Hailey glanced at him frustrated that he was pulling her attention away from weighing the pros and cons of the situation. "For what? I am trying to think here Jarrek.

Go find your brother and plan war with him. I need a few moments to think."

"Hailey, I am warning you. Come here to me." Jarrek called.

"Jarrek, you really don't want to take that tone with me. If I am frustrating you, then go find your brother." Hailey told him quite seriously.

"Hailey you are wasting time with your method. If you can just come over here for a few moments, I will show you a way to clear your thoughts and make an informed decision." Jarrek went from demanding to cajoling. He was learning a little about his mate and sometimes the high road would work better for him. He also needed to get his hands back on his mate in the worst way.

"Fine, Jarrek. It had better work, or I will kick you out of here so I can think. You're distracting." Hailey told him as she came to stand in front of him. Before she could tell him to get on with his demonstration, he turned her around and undid the ties to her gown in a blink. He turned her back to face him and the top of her gown fell forward exposing her breasts. He quickly pulled the tie around her waist and most of the gown dropped to her knees. Only the ties at her wrists kept the garment on her body and Jarrek took care of that before she could bend to scoop up the garment to cover herself.

"Whoa. What in the hell are you doing? This isn't the time to get freaky Jarrek. Right now, I want to rip my skin off, as I feel unclean. I'm nowhere close to the mood." Hailey protested, trying to cover her breasts and panties from his gaze.

"Relax little bird. I only thought to rub oils on your body at this time." Jarrek told her as he picked her up and deposited her on the bed. He did not understand why she kept trying to cover all her parts. He had seen all of her and every inch of her was lovely. Placing her face down Jarrek told her, "Just stay there for a moment while I get the oil."

"Oh, you mean a massage. That sounds wonderful." Hailey sighed, pillowing her head on her arms.

Relaxing into the mattress was tough right now. In the back of her mind, she was whimpering and crying for her momma. She was having a difficult time thinking about those eggs and the fact she was going to be a mother, because the scenes of her body being raped and violated had her wanting to vomit and burn all her skin off at the same time, which was adding to the shame running through her body.

She felt like she should be able to rise above this since she was gonna be a momma herself, but she had never expected to be one. She knew how her momma acted when someone threatened her. It was fierce and a little scary. She had a wonderful example in her momma's actions, so why was she having such a hard time deciding?

She felt Jarrek return and then the mattress dipped as he straddled her legs. She felt herself tense up. Why hadn't she covered herself up while he was gone? She was lying on the bed with nothing but her panties on. She really was losing her mind, if she was comfortable showing off the cellulite in her ass and thighs. She started to turn over so she could at least get her ass covered up, but Jarrek completely sat on her legs to stop her movement.

"Easy little bird. You are fine and I am just going to help you relax a little." He could already see the tension in her body. Watching that message had been a mistake. He could see that now. He only wanted to know how to handle the Krakill eggs with her genetic makeup. She had insisted on watching those horrible scenes. She had handled herself better than he thought.

He was quite proud of the indomitable spirit she showed in adversity. She would need it when she was his Queen, but some acts of violence did not need witnessing. Varill had been uncharacteristically kind in not letting her feel or remember her rape. That was the only thing for which Jarrek was grateful. Now it would be his job to take her away from those images. He should have just spanked her ass when she had gotten demanding.

Smoothing oil on her back in long smooth strokes, he made sure to cover her

entire back, shoulders and arms. Pouring
more into his hand, he set the bottle aside
and briskly rubbed his hands together to heat
the oil. Once he felt the oil heated enough,
he started at the base of her spine and circled
up to her shoulders using firm circular
motions.

"Ohhhhh. God, Jarrek. That is sooo
good." Hearing her moan was wreaking
havoc with his cock, but he was determined
to concentrate on Hailey's pleasure.

Jarrek massaged her shoulders and
down each arm. Seeming to pull all the
tension right out of her body into her
fingertips and then away from her entirely.
He was a master and she was a pile of goo
under his hands.

"That feels so wonderful, Jarrek.
Thank you."

"Oh little bird. I am just getting
started." Jarrek told her and then slid further
down her body. Pulling her panties down
and off her body in a subtle move that barely
shifted his relaxed mate, Jarrek grabbed the
bottle of oil again. Drizzling the oil up both

legs and let a generous portion pool along the seam of her ass. Warming his hands, he started working on her calves and feet. Drawing moan, groans, sighs and gasps from her were like a melody to his ears. Her body was his instrument and he was learning to create a symphony for the ages.

He gently pulled apart her legs and worked on her thighs. Reaching the bottom of her beautiful ass, he slipped his thumbs along the lips of her pussy toward her little nub before he began to trace her lips back to her ass. Digging in his thumbs, he grabbed her cheeks and began to knead them, exposing her rosette to his hungry gaze. He would take her there one day. Not today, but in the very near future. His cock was in serious need of attention.

Right now Hailey only needed his love and attention. He would show her that he was right for her by showing her with his actions that no matter what was done to her body against her will; it would never change his undying devotion to her. She had said she felt unclean and wanted to scrub her skin off; he wanted to show her that she was perfect and unsullied by the rough treatment of Varill. A male, no matter the species, or size, had no right to seize by force. A hundred Krakill could have touched her body or even shoved their cocks into her and it would change nothing. It broke his heart, it made his blood boil and made him crave the blood of those who had harmed her, but she was his cherished little bird, and he would show her in his worship of her body.

Gently turning her over, her body so relaxed as to be near sleep, Jarrek began at her feet again and worked his way up. His movements were slow and easy, opening her legs and spreading the lips of her pussy to show the glistening dew of her arousal. The scent of her pussy drifted up to him and he paused a moment to take a deep breath. She smelled so wonderful. He had to taste her.

He was salivating at the idea of lapping the honey straight from her well. Lowering himself on to his stomach, he framed her cunt with his hands. She was almost hairless. Just a small patch of hair lay at the top of her pussy like a crown. Her lips were puffy and dark, wet with her arousal.

Gently pulling her lips open, he got his first look at the tender center. She was flushed a deep pink on the tips of her lips and went to a deep red at the center of her clit. He could feel his little bird stir when he blew hot air against her exposed clit.

"Um, Jarrek. I'm not really comfortable with you down there. I would prefer you let me have a shower first. I mean I don't really like oral pleasure. Sometimes I got a tingle, but for the most part I would rather give than receive." Trying to close her legs as she felt her cheeks heat up in embarrassment, Hailey tried to stop Jarrek from putting his face any closer to her pussy.

"I don't know the last time I was able to get a shower in, so I can't guarantee the freshness, ya know? God this is embarrassing. Thanks for the massage, really. I feel much better, but I would prefer to stop now." Hailey struggled to get into a position where she could sit up and close her legs completely, but she was stopped by Jarrek's tongue licking a path straight up her slit.

"Oh holy fuck!" Hailey exclaimed and fell back against the bed. His tongue felt amazing. Forget a little tingle. He had just given her a full-blown zing. "Well maybe you can do that for a few moments then." Hailey said as Jarrek parted her lips and tasted the inside of her pussy.

Jarrek had never tasted anything as wonderful as the honey Hailey produced. He was going to make her his main meal for the next eight thousand years. He spent several minutes just nibbling along her lips, making sure to touch every inch of her skin. He flicked her clit, and slid two fingers inside her cunt. She felt so smooth and silky, stretching his fingers in a V; he turned them around and crooked his fingers. He explored the contours of her cunt, loving how she squeezed his fingers.

It would be a tight fit when they joined, but he relished the idea of her muscles strangling his cock. He rubbed and touched the inside of her vagina, finding all the little places that made her moans increase, or made her wiggle to get deeper before pulling his fingers free. Sliding his hands under her ass, he tilted her cunt up to his tongue.

"I'm going to taste you deep now Hailey. I need to drink deep of your well. You are so delicious that my hunger is growing. Do you want me to put my tongue deep inside that beautiful pussy, little bird? Do you want to feed my hunger with your creamy cunt?"

Hailey was beginning to feel desperate. Her insides were on fire and she could feel the ball of tension getting tighter and tighter. He was going to make her scream soon. She just needed a little something more, "God Jarrek, yes. Taste my pussy deep. Oh please don't stop. I'm gonna come soon." Hailey cried, grabbing at Jarrek's head and trying to force him to keep going. "Just a little more."

Jarrek loved the feel of Hailey's nails digging deep into his scalp. The way she was almost ripping his hair out to get him to continue. It amped up his own pleasure, he was going to have to get relief after she came, or his cock would explode. Bending his head to Hailey's dripping pussy, he circled her clit with his forefinger. Without actually touching her sensitive nub, he kept lightly circling her clit. Stabbing his tongue deep in her pussy, he imitated what he would like to do to her with his cock and then pinched her clit hard.

As soon as Hailey began to scream out her orgasm, he pulled his tongue from her pussy and sucked her clit into his mouth as though he would swallow it completely. Giving her clit the occasional flick with his tongue, he kept her riding the crest of the orgasm. Once she began to whimper, showing that it was too sensitive, he stabbed his tongue back into the well of her cunt and lapped at all the cream she had made for him.

Once he had gotten as much of her cream as possible, Jarrek went up to his knees and ripped open his trousers. Freeing his cock from the tight confines of his armor felt so good he gave a little groan of relief. Sliding the fingers of his left hand into her pussy, he got his fingers full of her honey and used it to lubricate his straining cock. It was rigid with the veins distended, pulsing with the heat of his arousal. Five rough tugs and he shouted his own release. His release was so strong it splashed long strings, from her breasts to the top of her thighs.

After Jarrek and caught his breath, he stood and stripped out of his clothes. Picking his sated Cordisa up into his arms, he took them both to the cleansing room.

"Come on little bird, let's get you cleaned up." Activating the red sterilization field, he directed her attention to the red haze surrounding them.

"The red haze is actually an ultra violet free solar beam that will burn off dead skin and then sterilize your body by removing any contaminants. There is no need to remove your lovely skin, as this will leave you completely clean. The oil I used earlier will act as a cleanser as well. In just a few more seconds when the red turns to white, you can step out knowing you are clean."

"Wow. We immerse ourselves in hot steaming water with oils, foaming cleanser or just the water itself. We let the heat loosen our muscles and help with any aches from injuries. We also use it to relax and get our thoughts organized. We call it either bubble bath, for the foaming cleanser, or just a bath. We also have cubicles like this that have a showerhead that pours water out of it to simulate rainfall. Then we put the cleanser on little scrubbing cloths to run all over our bodies to help remove the dirt and dead skin cells. Then we rinse off the soap and use a different type of cleanser on our heads. Women like to condition their hair as the cleanser tends to leave it very dry. We rinse again before we are done. We call this showering. Your process sure is easier." Hailey explained to Jarrek as once the light turned to white, he stepped out and created new clothing for her.

This was a simpler gown in turquoise, as it gathered at one shoulder with a diamond clasp, leaving her other shoulder bare. It lifted her breasts somehow, so that there was no need for a bra and then cinched at her hips before falling to her ankles. He produced some glittery sandals with a two-inch heel for her before pulling out another black form suit for himself. "I will need to head back to the bridge. I will have Sidhawk entertain you and show you around the ship. He can also make sure you get something to eat. He will allow no harm to come to you while I am gone, but I do not anticipate any trouble at this time." He told her as he finished dressing.

Pulling her into his arms, he took a few moments to kiss her and hold her, before telling her, "I will call you to the bridge in a few hours to see if you have made your decision and to tell you of any plans I have made. Until then know that you hold my soul. I cannot wait until I can bond us together for all time." Placing one last kiss on her shoulder, he strode from the room.

9.

How Many People Saw

That?

"Bond?" she whispered to the empty room. A few moments later the door opened again as Sidhawk returned to keep her company. He had managed to clean up and change clothes. He also looked more subdued than when he left. "What's wrong Sid?" Hailey asked.

"I went to see Kirrek to discover what was wrong and saw what had been done to you and my Prince. I quickly went to cleanse myself and change into my armor. I am not a warrior like Kirrek or the Prince, but I can fight and protect you. My body can shield yours. Our armor can take more damage than your fragile body."

Hailey shrank away from Sidhawk. "You saw that? Why? How many damn people have seen my shame? I want that message restricted right now, Sidhawk. Call Jarrek right now!" Hailey's voice grew in volume at the end until she was practically screaming.

"Whoa, Hailey. Calm down. It is not your shame. How can you say that? No one who has seen that message has blamed you for what happened. How could we? We place the blame right where it belongs on the hated Varill. If you will please calm down I will comm Jarrek and Kirrek right now and you can talk to Jarrek yourself. You will see that nothing you did was wrong." Sidhawk tried to lower his voice and speak in soothing tones. He did not like the panicked expression on Hailey's face. Her face had looked so relaxed and happy when he had walked in. He would let Jarrek kick his ass if he became angry with him for upsetting his Cordisa. Picking up the comm, he quickly reached Jarrek and explained that he had upset Hailey after telling her that he had seen the message. Handing the comm out, Hailey put it to her ear and started in on Jarrek.

"Jarrek I don't want anyone else to see my shame. Do you hear me? No one else needs to see what happened to me. People will look down on me or treat me weird." Hailey yelled at Jarrek.

"Little bird, listen to me. I will pull the message right off the board right now. I will put it in the restricted section for the Captain's eyes only. Will that make you feel better?" Jarrek asked.

"Yes. But I want you to make sure the people who saw it keep their mouths shut. I don't like people knowing those bad things happened to me, and I sure as hell don't want 'em gossiping about me like little old ladies in a Bible belt town." Hailey wanted some kind of reassurance from Jarrek that his men could keep a lid on their mouths.

"Hailey, my men would never talk about what happened to you like that. They are all honorable men, and those who were on the bridge to see the message are still here. I will personally tell each of them, that if they repeat to anyone else what they saw in that message, I will eviscerate them where they stand. If you like, I will take a blood vow on the matter." Jarrek assured his mate. If someone upset her then he would kill them. Simple as that.

Hailey gave a little internal eye roll at the offer to take a blood vow. Men were such strange creatures. "No Jarrek, I don't require a blood vow from you. Your word is enough for me. Just make sure that you pull the video right now. My shame is my own to deal with and not for others to enjoy the viewing of." The snark in her voice was completely lost on Jarrek. Hell even Sidhawk didn't get it. Aliens. Well, they were sexy.

"You say shame, when there is none Hailey. Not one little bit of shame falls on your shoulders. Men, no matter the species, who take by force are cowards and should be executed on sight. Do you hear me, Hailey? I will not have you believe yourself shamed. I have tried to show you that I still love and desire you. Did I do such a bad job, that I need to repeat it? I will be happy to come back and repeat it as much as you need." Jarrek teased her.

"No. I got it. Just remove the video. I'll get it together on my end. Thanks Jarrek." Hailey assured him. She didn't need him to come distract her, he did a good enough job of that without him right there. Handing the comm to Sidhawk, she turned her back to him and walked to the small table in the food prep area.

"So what's to eat in this joint? I'm starving and food helps me think." She asked casually, trying to move on from knowing that he had seen her naked and violated.

"I have many delicacies that I can make for you. Do you have a taste for anything in particular?" Sidhawk asked, happy to move on.

"I somehow doubt you have grilled cheese sandwiches and Doritos in the cupboard, huh?" Hailey asked doubtfully.

"Just make me a couple of your favorites and I will try to see if something is to my tastes."

"Do you have any questions for me while I get you something to eat? Something on your mind that I could help with?" Sidhawk asked from the prep counter.

"Well unless you can tell me whether I should try to save the eggs incubated with my genetic material or have Jarrek kill them, then I could maybe think of a few questions I have." Hailey tried to joke. It fell flat, but she tried. She gave herself points for that.

"I don't see how that would be possible, Hailey as they actually have specific needs at specific times and this is instinctive to the sire that is incubating. They have an almost telekinetic link with the young in the egg and the young wouldn't be able to survive the loss of the father." Sidhawk said so matter of fact, that it surprised Hailey.

"What? Then if this is known, why did Jarrek even ask me?" Hailey questioned.

"Well, it is not something that is widely known. I have been studying the Krakill over the last ten years. At every port we stop in, I make it a point to travel to the sectors medical area. Krakill's are tolerated only on trade planets, moons and asteroids under strict watch. They are known throughout the universe for their knowledge in genetics and medical training. They congregate in these areas and discuss their knowledge; they have even traded on that knowledge for supplies that they require. I inquire about what they did or said, just ask questions. When I felt I had enough information, I was going to share it with the Commander. I was not keeping it a secret exactly; it just seemed smart to learn all I could so as to try to find a way to kill them quicker. I worry for Kirrek sometimes. There have been a many instances over the last fifty years when he almost died in his pursuit to eradicate their species. I know we are a dying race, but I would like as much time with my friend as possible before he goes to greet the Goddess. It was about twelve years ago that I almost lost him completely. He struggled for a year to get back to fighting form. I helped nurse him through that time. I watched as he struggled to return to fight and I decided I would study them." Sidhawk finished with a shrug as though it was no big deal.

Hailey looked at him and shook her head. "That is smart. Why are you the only one to have thought of it? I would think since you have been trying to kill the Krakill's for some time now, that somewhere along the way, someone would have said, "Well how are they fashioned? Can we kill them with extreme heat or cold? How can we better kill large numbers of them? How can we keep them from reproducing at all?" and then created a committee to research and answer those questions. That's one of the first things we would've done back on Earth." Hailey actually felt relieved over his information. She just didn't think she could have handled a bunch of lizard-alligator looking egg children.

She would have loved them as they were a part of her, but it would have been a struggle to understand them and help them grow and develop. She could cry and mourn them when she was alone, but it helped her to know she wouldn't have been able to save them.

"Well, that helps end my anguish over the eggs. You really should pass everything you know about them along to Jarrek or Kirrek if you don't feel comfortable telling your Commander."

Sidhawk set several dishes in front of Hailey and she took a deep breath of each one. If it stank too badly, she would pass on those. To her surprise, everything smelled wonderful, so she dug in. She was quite happy to fill her growling stomach. Hailey was a little uncomfortable having him watch her eat, so she paused long enough to say, "You can help me eat some of this if you're hungry. I was also wondering about the bonding thing Jarrek mentioned. What did he mean?"

"You are a Cordisa to Jarrek. This means that you alone are to be the other half of his heart and soul. Someone to help complete him, someone he can love without reserve, have children, and grow old with.

When we find our Cordisa or Corduva then
we bond our life forces together to fully
immerse ourselves into one cohesive being.
He will give you a part of his essence and
symbiot's life force and tie you together.
You will understand one another on a level
you would not be able to reach without the
bond. You will know when he is hurt,
whether emotionally or physically. He will
know how to please you as well. The bond
means a deeper understanding of one
another. Your heart, mind, secrets, joy, pain.
All of it will be known and shared. You
could close your eyes and pinpoint where he
is and if he is okay with a thought. If you
were close to, dying Jarrek could morph to
your side in a microsecond and morph you
to safety and the same is true for you. If his
life force was slipping away, you could use
the bond to get him to safety. You would not
be capable of carrying him, but as long as
you got your arms around him, you could
morph to safety. We normally require some
time to recoup our energies when we morph;
however, bonded mates have a hundred
times the energy as unmated males do. No
one but bonded mates can explain all that

the energy does as it seems to be different for each couple." Sidhawk gave a little deprecating laugh.

"Perhaps this is a question best answered by your Corduva. I am afraid that I am not doing a very good job."

Hailey swallowed one last bite before pushing her plate away. She may have started out starving, but the more that Sidhawk explained about the bond the more that she disliked the idea of bonding. The thought that there would be nothing private, nothing she could keep hidden. No thanks. There were horrible things in her past that no one needed to know. She hadn't even shared them with her momma and there wasn't much she didn't tell her.

Also, everyone had thoughts both good and bad that they kept to themselves. People were complicated. You could be polite, but think horrible thoughts in your head, or use a celebrity to help get off when your partner wasn't hitting the right notes, been hurt or angry and hid it. The list of things we kept hidden from one another was endless. She couldn't imagine being so open and vulnerable to someone. It actually made her nauseous.

"How do you bond? Is there a ceremony, does he have to bite me, or what?" Hailey asked with what she hoped was a curious tone of voice instead of how she was actually feeling.

Sidhawk smiled at her, but answered her question. "No he doesn't have to bite you. We do have a ceremony for joining, but it can be done before or after the bonding takes place. To bond he will make love to all of your body. Once he has tasted of your honey, the one after he has given you an orgasm, he will then need to give you his essence in your mouth and anal cavities before he makes love to you from behind and then right as he reaches climax he will latch onto the nap of your neck and kiss you. He must have given you his seed in each area first. Why? Do you have to bite him for you to join life forces?" He asked curiously.

"No, on my planet we only have a wedding ceremony when two people want to join their lives together. They have a priest or judge preside over a ceremony where they pledge in front of friends and family that they will love one another in sickness and health, for richer or poorer until death they do part. Then after they exchange rings and a kiss, the priest or judge tells everyone that they are joined together as husband and wife. They have a party and then they go on a honeymoon for two weeks to someplace where they can be secluded together and have lots of sex." Hailey told him while thinking how she was going to find a way to avoid bonding sex with Jarrek.

"Um one more question about this. Does he have to do the bonding sex at the same time or could it be spread over days and weeks?" Hailey didn't want to panic if there was no need. He had already tasted her honey, but that was all. Thank god that they had been interrupted or she had fallen asleep before they kept going. She could have been mated before she knew it.

"Well, it can be done in stages, but why would a couple want that? When you find your Cordisa, everything else fades into the background. She consumes your thoughts and actions. Only in times like now, when Jarrek must concentrate on killing Varill does a bonding get postponed or broken up into sections."

Sidhawk tried to explain the process, but knew he was doing a poor job. He could not understand why she asked if it could be broken up, until he realized that perhaps she worried that Jarrek did not want to bond her to him. That is why he mentioned that only in this situation it could happen. He could definitely help ease her mind if that was the case.

"I assure you Hailey, Jarrek is quite anxious to complete your bonding. Only because he wants to protect you is he not with you here now." Sidhawk smiled to her, quite pleased with himself that he could ease her worry.

Hailey looked at him and said, "Then I better figure out how to keep from getting bonded."

That wiped the smile right off of his face. Surely, he misunderstood her. The language was a little tough. Perhaps his translator was malfunctioning. As he was about to question her, the comm rang and Jarrek requested their presence on the bridge.

10.

Almost Bonded

She was quite impressed with the ship as Sidhawk led her down the corridor to the elevator that he called a lift. The floor was a soft cushion of a rubbery like substance. It apparently was waterproof and fire proof. It also was self-cleaning. Apparently, the rubber was actually skin that sucked up dirt or anything that fell on it to nourish itself. It would consume the trash and uneaten meals from the crew. She didn't ask what it secreted as its waste. Some things are better unknown and unasked.

The walls were a lemony yellow and quite soothing. When she questioned Sidhawk about the color choice, his answer certainly surprised her. Yellow was a

traditional color to give a couple who had
just given birth to a child so they associated
the color with babies, which helped the big
bad warriors relax. Necessary when you
have thousands crammed inside a metal
ship, no matter how vast. It may have been
quite a long while since they had even
witnessed a child's birth, but the color still
worked.

The lift was so smooth she never felt
it move. They had stepped in and the door
had closed. Sidhawk had said bridge and
then a few moments later the door opened
again. Walking onto the bridge with
Sidhawk, she remembered that these
warriors had seen her violation and she was
both embarrassed and angry.

They all looked at her, and all though
no one said anything about what they had
seen, she felt compelled to add her own
warning to these men. Raising her chin, she
looked over the room and said very clearly,
"I will castrate any man here who mentions
what they have seen in the message from
Varill. I don't care what you think of me
because of it, but you will not repeat those

thoughts. If I find out, I will make it my personal mission to see you live a life of pain and agony. I will make sure that before Jarrek kills you, you will pray to all the gods you had kept your tongue still. If for some reason you do not understand the word castrate, let me tell you just what that means. Your male sac, the one that holds the testicles, and the sperm needed for procreation is tied and then cut off in this process. It helps male animals lose their aggression. I however, will not just cut off your man sac but your rod as well. I hope I am understood."

Hailey watched as many of them grabbed their crotch and kept her laugh inside her head. They all vowed silence and bowed to her. Hailey then glanced around for Jarrek. "Where is his high and mighty self?"

Jarrek, who had been coming out of his conference room, saw Hailey stop just inside the entrance. He was about to go to her side and lead her to his conference room, when she lifted her chin and threatened his men. His chest swelled with pride at her actions, and he winced when she defined her term of castrate. Of course, he would help her if his men hurt her feelings, but he was male and could not help but not cringe in sympathy at the thought. Most of his men covered their manhood from even the suggestion.

"I am here little bird." Jarrek called out and went to take her in his arms. He was proud that his men all vowed to keep the message private, not that he had a doubt, but they could have been offended at her accusation.

"Why would you call me high? I know that I am mighty and I am glad that you recognize that, but I do not think I understand your meaning. Come into the conference room and we can make some plans." Jarrek said as he led her away.

Hailey looked back at Sidhawk and said, "Don't you think you should come with me and tell them what you know." She had no problem throwing Sidhawk into the hot seat. Jarrek probably wouldn't like her explanation of high and mighty so she needed Sidhawk to deflect his ire.

"You have information, warrior Barion? You will join me now and explain." Jarrek ordered with narrowed eyes. He had always thought Sidhawk to be a good influence on Kirrek, but if he were holding out, he would have to rethink that and have him watched.

"Jeez Jarrek, don't take that tone with Sid. This tone right there is why I called you high and mighty. It means someone who thinks more of himself than is prudent or warranted, very bossy and domineering." Hailey told Jarrek, surprised that he would treat his brother's lover like that. She tried to ignore the guffaws coming from the men behind and in front of her when she told Jarrek the definition.

"It is fine Hailey. Of course I will come and give my information to my Prince." Sidhawk told Hailey.

Looking to Jarrek, he continued with, "When I had completed my study I would have let either Kirrek or you know first,

Commander. I did not realize this was something that needed immediate sharing, until I was talking with your Cordisa over a meal. Unfortunately, she had not gotten to finish that meal when summoned here. If you could have some provisions brought up for her I will tell you all I know."

Sidhawk promised his Prince. If Jarrek was angry with him, he was happy to answer any questions put to him. He was touched though, that Hailey defended him. She was going to make and excellent Queen.

"I have provisions set on the table, as I was unaware if she had gotten a chance to eat or not. I was originally going to call for her in two hours. Giving her plenty of time to see some of the ship and have a meal. However, new developments are pushing for action sooner rather than later. I give you apologies Sidhawk; I would have had you come in as well as unfortunately, one of those developments involves my hot-headed brother." Jarrek advised as he led them into the room and secured the door. There were five warriors seated around a table laden with a banquet of food. They were silent as

Jarrek led her and Sidhawk into the room and she wondered if she needed to repeat her warning to these men or if they had heard her through the open door. Although she doubted it, as they all had little smiles on their faces as they tried to contain their laughter from her berating Jarrek.

"Goddess, save me." Sidhawk whispered. Louder he said, "Let me guess. He did not wait around for a clear plan to be made, but took two or three men on a stealth mission that failed? He is either dead or being tortured and held for your good behavior?"

He bowed his head and pinched the bridge of his nose. Goddesses save him from ignorant, hotheaded, sexy, pain-in-the-ass warriors. He did not know how much more of this he could take. They had a deep love, true, but he was tired of watching Kirrek try to kill himself.

Jarrek seated Hailey and began to put together a plate for her to eat, trying to give Sidhawk a minute to collect himself, as he had regrettably called the situation correctly.

"Try this vishna. I have a home on our moon that makes this concoction. Careful though. I had Sameth check if you could eat all of this, as I did not wish to poison you and he said that your body will tolerate all of this, but that the vishna may affect your libido and inhibitions." Jarrek told her and took a seat next to her.

"Hailey, go ahead and start eating and I will go around the room and introduce you to the others I have gathered here."

Jarrek cleared his throat and began. "Starting to your right, I would like to introduce to you, Warrior first class, Bruthus M'et Fornon. He is a stealth pilot and captain of his own team of fighter pilots. Next to him, you have Warrior second class, Marthos R'et Barion, cousin to me and younger brother to Sameth. He is an experienced sniper and usually covers us on our missions."

Before Jarrek moved forward with the next introduction, Marthos broke in with, "That is probably why you were captured Commander. However, I guess you still got lucky, since you met this captivating creature. If you need any help kicking his ass, you call me and let me know beautiful woman. I will be happy to help." Marthos winked at her and let her know with his eyes, he liked what he saw.

Jarrek growled low in his throat at the look in his cousin's eye. "Marthos you may not live long enough to keep that oath. Keep your heated eyes off my Hailey or I will remove them."

Pulling Hailey's chair a little closer to his, he continued. "Moving on, we have twin brothers, Warriors first class, and expert assassins Heathrick and Shemrick G'el Trion. Each warrior raised his hand to his heart and gave her a small bow from the waist. I can only tell them apart by calling their names. Whomever lifts his head first is usually Heathrick. They do not say much, but that works, as they need to be invisible enough to get close to the enemy. Finally, I would like to introduce you to Elite Warrior Rometho Q'el Trindon. He is an expert in explosives and older brother to Loku, who is my second in command. He is the best we have and I wanted you to meet him."

Jarrek finished the introductions, and then turned back to Sidhawk. "If you are ready warrior Barion, perhaps we can start with what information you gave to my Cordisa?"

Hailey ate from the plate that Jarrek had filled for her, and let her gaze wander over all the warriors that he had introduced as Sidhawk went through all the information he had managed to learn about the Krakill.

She had heard the most important part, to her situation anyway, and wanted to try to file the faces of these warriors in her head while the introductions were fresh in her mind. They were all huge even seated and wearing the same version of uniform as Jarrek, but they all looked so different. Drinking deeply of her wine, or vishna, as Jarrek called it she began looking them over in the manner that Jarrek introduced them.

Bruthus looked the oldest; although how she was supposed to know for sure, with how long they lived, she would never know. He was the one that had the most lines on his face though. Being a captain of a group of fighter pilot's must be stressful if the lines were any indication. He had obsidian and copper eyes that didn't shine like Jarrek's did. Truthfully, he looked a little sad. He had very short hair that hugged his scalp and didn't look over a half-inch long. His forehead had deep worry or pain lines, but his brows were the most interesting feature on his face. He had one brow that arched perfectly and one that looked cut in half where an inch wide scar dissected it. It ended just under his right eye in a round scar like the end of an exclamation point. His nose was bumpy and scarred over. His lower lip was fuller than his upper lip, but his mouth wasn't very wide. Lines dug into his mouth giving him a pinched expression. It was an interesting face, but he needed someone who could help erase the tension and pain.

Sameth's brother Marthos was a bit of a clown with his flirting and trying to get under his cousins skin. He may think she was sexy, but he would never act on it.

Those who spent a lot of time joking were covering up something else. Make people laugh to hide the hurt, or make them dismiss what the real problem was. She would keep an eye on Marthos to see if there was something, she could do to help him. Like Sameth, his hair was a golden-blonde, although he wore his in intricate braids pulled away from his face. His eyes were also like Sameth's with their shimmering obsidian and gold, but the glint in his eyes was more serious and did not make her relax.

The twins were a type of gorgeous that anyone would describe in bold, capital letters. Words like "Sex Walking!" or "Panty Melting!" even "Orgasms 'R Us!" fit them. How they could be assassins was beyond her. They would stand out where ever they went. Dark blonde hair with brown and auburn highlights brushed their broad shoulders with muscles that strained their suit. They were the first of their kind that had eyes that were a little more familiar to her. They had a deep turquoise color almost as hypnotizing as Jarrek's. They could put any Hollywood bad boy to shame. A full brow rose above those turquoise eyes outlined in a thin line of black as if to highlight just how unique they really were. They had long straight noses, with full, lick-able, kissable lips. She was quite glad that Jarrek couldn't read her mind as she was seriously wondering what she would look like between them. She squirmed a little in her seat, hoping that she wouldn't leave a wet spot when she stood up. She noticed that the only way to tell them apart was what hand they used. Heathrick favored his left hand and Shemrick favored his right. They had given her the heart salute with bow that all these warriors favored when Jarrek introduced them.

Rometho was the last warrior introduced, but he was still a gorgeous man. His hair was in a more traditional style. If she were on earth, she wouldn't be surprised to find him on the cover of Forbes or GQ. His black hair parted to the right and back off his forehead. His brows only had a slight arch and his lashes were the thickest she had seen among those she had met. It made his obsidian and rust colored eyes look darker than they probably were, giving him a smoldering, sexy look. His lips were full, with the bottom just a little plumper. It was like he wore a permanent come fuck me look. He wasn't as thickly muscled as the twins were, but he was still quite muscular. He was another one that left her panting and wondering what he would look like naked. She was turning into quite the slut and loving it. Sidhawk was finished with his Intel and she hoped that there wasn't anything crucial for her to know in there.

Hailey looked down at her plate, trying to get her mind back on business and not on seeing if she could instigate an orgy. She also noticed her glass was empty. "Thanks, Sid. Now let's see what we can do to get your honey's ass out of the frying pan."

Looking over at Jarrek, she asked for more vishna and then turned to the other warriors. "All right guys, what's the plan to get Mr. Hot-head back from his misadventure and kill the bad guys?"

Jarrek handed her another glass of wine and began with, "Well I have been in talks with Rometho about explosives to place in the ship, something good enough that it makes the ship collapse in on itself and completely kills all on board. Heathrick and Shemrick will find and rescue our daughter, with as little fuss as possible. Bruthus will fly us in his test shuttle, and if all works as it should, we should be completely undetectable. He will then help Rometho place the explosives. Unfortunately, we were interrupted by the message that Kirrek had pulled his disappearing act and Varill was calling to whine about Kirrek and show all the bruises and cuts that he was adding to Kirrek's body. He then gave me only five hours to give you up to him." Jarrek finished and leaned back in his seat and finished off the vishna.

"We also need to find a way to keep our daughter alive when they do find her. I hope you have a plan for that. You know I never thought I would be a mom. Hope I'm a good one and don't give her a complex." Hailey mused. All the men assured her she would make a lovely mother. She blinked tears from her eyes and thanked them all.

"Heathrick and Shemrick, do you have enough med skills to do so?" Hailey questioned. When they shook their heads in the negative, she turned to Jarrek and told him, "Sameth needs to be a part of the mission to keep our daughter alive. I think you should go ahead and do it."

He looked over at her with a tender expression. "Do what, little bird?" he asked.

"I think you should call Varill up and tell him you will do it. You'll trade me for your brother." Hailey said.

All the men jumped out of their chairs and called out their denials, except Jarrek. He leaned close to her and cupped her face with one hand and told her quite seriously, "I am about to put you over my knee and spank your ass, little bird. There is no way that you are going into danger."

"That is not what I meant. Let me explain first Jarrek, before you blow me off. I meant that you tell Varill that you will do it, but then send off the team to get in place before our arrival. They place the explosives; Heathrick and Shemrick rescue Kirrek, and Marthos and Sameth can find our daughter and carefully transfer her to the shuttle. Then we make a big fuss and dock with Varill's ship and while they are getting away, you can say that you changed your mind and he can keep Kirrek as your gift to him, but that you prefer pussy anyway. We break away and start racing back to your ship and Rometho can set off the explosives, blowing all of them to hell. Then we can all go to earth and my momma will cook you up some southern food that is so good your stomach will want to explode from how much you have stuffed into it."

She cleared her throat and then turned to Jarrek and said before she thought about it, "Besides, was that threat supposed to scare me? My pussy is so hot right now; I would probably cream your uniform so much you would need to change your clothes." Hailey then put her hand over her mouth. Whoa. That was supposed to be only inside her head. "I meant you and whose army. There is no way I will let you spank me like a child." Hailey tried to correct, but the volume came out small and weak.

Jarrek just smiled and slowly stood up. "I want all of you to leave me and my little bird now." When they continued to sit there for a few moments, he bellowed, "OUT!" in his loudest roar. That caused Hailey to jump and all of his warriors to chuckle and file out of the conference room. Watching all of the guys leave her alone with Jarrek, she stood to leave as well. Slowly, she inched around the table, while keeping her eyes on Jarrek.

"I think I am going to go find my room too if you don't mind. I need the bathroom and a nap if we are going to rescue our daughter and your brother." Hailey told him as she was almost around the table and close to the door. Before she could blink, Jarrek had her in his arms, was pushing plates and food out of the way, and he was placing her face down on the table. With her legs, dangling over the side Hailey cried out, "Wait Jarrek, you don't want to do this. I promise you don't."

"Oh, little bird. You have no idea how badly I have wanted to do this. I wanted to spank your delectable ass when you pulled that absurd escape from your cage." Jarrek told her as he easily held her in place and lifted her gown. Once he exposed her ass to his gaze, he continued chastising her. "I would have helped you escape, but you took matters into your own hands and risked your life. You need me to help keep you from making poor decisions. I think a count of fifteen will help you learn the error of your ways. Would you like to count them out for me, little bird, or would you prefer that I count for you?" Jarrek asked as he pulled her panties off and gently rubbed his hand across her ass.

Hailey tried to kick out at Jarrek, but he had her pinned with his body leaving little room for her to do much damage. "I will not count for you, you big jerk! You really need to stop Jarrek. I don't want this." Hailey screamed and pleaded.

Jarrek opened Hailey's thighs just enough so that he could slip two fingers into her pussy. Pushing them deep and then pulling them out to show her how wet she was. "I think that you do my little bird. I do not mind counting for you." Jarrek said, and then let his hand fall on her right cheek. Rubbing it a little to help spread the pain out, he listened to her high scream of "Ow! That really hurt dammit! That's enough Jarrek."

"I agree. There is no need to scream like that yet Hailey. Be a good girl and take your punishment." Jarrek told her before he gave her three more smacks in quick succession. Making sure to get each cheek and spread them out over her ass.

"That is four little bird. Let us check your temperature." Hailey was sobbing and telling him no, but they were weak and he knew she did not mean it. He slipped his fingers back into her pussy giving her several deep thrusts. She was dripping so much honey he scooped some onto his fingers and licked them clean.

"Hmm, you taste delicious Hailey, and I love the rose color of your plush ass. You were definitely made for me." So saying he gave her six more smacks, putting a little more power behind them. The last two he aimed at the seam of her ass and thigh. Hailey was crying and wiggling against the table and pleading with him to stop.

"Little bird, the count now is ten. You only have to take five more and I will give you your reward."

"I don't know if I can do five more Jarrek. Something feels strange and my stomach is starting to feel weird." Hailey sobbed. Her ass was on fire and she felt a pressure building inside her that was scaring her a little as it was not something she had ever felt before. Her clit felt like exploding, it throbbed and pulsed with every strike from Jarrek's hand.

"Oh, little bird. Have you never had your beautiful ass spanked?" Jarrek asked her.

Hailey took a moment to sniffle back her tears, and answered, "No."

"I know what you need Hailey. I will take care of you always my love." Jarrek said and spread her legs wide apart and put her knees on the table. Leaving her wide open to anything he wanted to do to her and pulling her pussy up and off the table. Rubbing her cheeks and the lips of her pussy, Jarrek held back only a little as he smacked each cheek twice and then slapped her pussy right at her distended clit. Hailey's chest came up off the table and the high keening cry of her orgasm echoed off the walls in an aria of perfect pitch.

Jarrek continued playing with her pussy as she squirted her cream all over his table. After her beautiful song wound down, she slumped back to the table, exhausted and more languid. Scooping up the proof of her orgasm, he used her cream to help lubricate her ass. Slowly he slipped a finger in past her ring of muscles. Hailey was so relaxed from the orgasm he had just given her that she barely tightened on his finger. Getting more cream from her pussy, he slipped in a second finger, getting a weak objection from

Hailey as she became aware of what he was doing.

"Shhh, little bird. I will take care of you." Jarrek promised as he spread his fingers to help stretch the guardian muscle of her ass. Slowly pushing them in and out, as he loosened her for the invasion of his cock.

"How does that feel Hailey? Am I hurting you little bird or are you just uncomfortable because you have never had your ass fucked?" Jarrek questioned.

An alarm started going off in the back of her head, but she couldn't concentrate on what it was trying to telling her for the strange sensations that Jarrek was causing. No one had ever asked her for anal sex, so she had never tried it, but the sensations that Jarrek gave her were making her body tingle. With the pain in her ass, and now a tingle throughout her body, she was confused as to what exactly she was feeling.

"It doesn't hurt. It, well it is making me tingle all over my body." Hailey answered.

"Let me know if you start to feel pain and I will go slower, little bird." Jarrek said before he used his other hand to spread her ass open a little more so he could bend over, lick and tease her hole with his tongue. Making sure to get her very wet. Keeping it slow and steady, he used two fingers to help stretch her for him.

Straightening up Jarrek dipped his free hand into Hailey's pussy, fucking her ass and pussy in tandem. The little mewls of pleasure coming from Hailey had him ready to burst, but she was not ready for his cock yet. Pulling his hand from her pussy, Jarrek slowly slipped a finger to join the two he had in her ass, making sure to stretch her open slowly as his other hand went in and out on a slow slide. His third finger was seated in her ass as far as it would go, so he sped up his movements and stretched her further for longer periods.

Once he felt that she was ready, he pulled his fingers from her ass entirely. Hailey objected to that quite loudly and Jarrek quickly ripped open his trousers and soothed Hailey by playing with her clit, while scooping up Hailey's cream so that he could coat his cock in her lubrication as fast as possible. Jarrek wanted to make sure that he did not hurt her, so he added some of his own spit. Placing the head of his cock against Hailey's hole, he told Hailey, "I'm going to sink my cock in your ass now, little bird. Push out against me as I push in. If it hurts at any time I want you to let me know."

Making sure to take it slow, even though he felt as though he could go off at any moment, Jarrek praised Hailey as she followed his directions and pushed out against him.

"Goddess, Hailey. You are so tight and warm. You feel so good. Such a beautiful little bird to take my cock in your ass. I wish you could see how sexy you look right now. I am having a hard time going slow as watching my cock sink into your ass is the most amazing event of my life."

Hailey felt the tingles race up and down her body in a continual loop as though it was an electric current. She knew that she wasn't supposed to do this, but couldn't remember why, and when Jarrek had licked her hole and used his fingers on her pussy and ass at the same time, she no longer cared why it wasn't such a good idea. The tingles just keep increasing and if they stopped so would she. It was like that was the only thing keeping her alive and breathing.

Then he had done just that and her verbal protestations had helped to get him to start back up. He was giving her instructions on how to take his cock and she was quite eager to follow them. If she had known that anal sex would feel this amazing, she would have started years ago. Jarrek was a lot bigger than the fingers he had used to prepare her, but the little pinch of pain actually ramped her desire up more.

When the ache became stronger, she took a deep breath and gave a small whimper. Trying to tell him in actual words felt more than she was capable of in that moment. She felt as though he was boiling her down to a primal being, all feeling and animal lust.

Jarrek was talking dirty to her, letting her know what he was feeling and how good it was and she loved it. When he asked if he was hurting her, she wanted to laugh, but couldn't. She wanted him to go faster; she wanted to feel all of him in her. She needed it more than air. She tried to verbalize it, but wasn't honestly sure she could. All that would come out was, "No hurt, need more. Give all. Faster. Deeper. Need. Hurry."

Jarrek heard Hailey's answer and even understood all she did not say. Thanking the Goddess for the gift that was Hailey, he allowed the tight grip he had on himself to fall away. Allowing his instincts and Hailey's grunts, moans and breathless, "yes, yes, yes." to be his guide. He gripped her shoulders and pulled her back on his cock faster and faster. She was a natural and seemed to follow his rhythm easily, squeezing his cock in a tight grip on the out stokes, pushing out on the in. They were one primal animal in the quest for fulfillment. Feeling the tingle start in his spine, he knew he was not going to last much longer.

Reaching under Hailey with his right hand, he rubbed her clit in tight hard circles. Keeping his grip on her left shoulder, he increased his pulls back, drilling his hips up to drive his cock a little deeper. Hailey's voice rose in volume and Jarrek began slapping at her clit. As soon as he felt the first tight squeeze on his cock from her orgasm, he grabbed her hips and pulled her back against him in fast tight thrusts. His last thought before letting his own orgasm swallow him whole, was he really loved Hailey's voice in orgasm and wondered if she would let him record it.

Jarrek was the first to recover and slowly pulled free of Hailey's warm haven. He was reluctant to leave as she had felt so good, but he knew he needed to get his little bird cleaned up. Grabbing a few of the cloth napkins from the banquet on the table, he cleaned himself off and then did the same for Hailey, before lowering her gown. Tossing the napkins aside, Jarrek searched for another bottle of vishna. He was so very thirsty. Finding Hailey's panties, he stuffed them in the seam of his trousers, before continuing his search. Finally, he found a bottle and opened it up. Assuming that Hailey would be as thirsty as he was, he poured her a large glass, before drinking straight from the bottle. Walking over to his beautiful love, he helped her sit up straight and handed her the glass of vishna.

"I figured you were probably thirsty too."

Hailey grabbed the glass and quickly downed the contents. He was right. She felt as dry as the Sahara. She still felt ready for more, though.

"Come, my love. That idea of a quick nap before we begin our plans for war sounds wonderful." Jarrek picked Hailey up in his arms, not quite ready to let her go he grabbed the last bottle of vishna and strode from the bridge, back to their quarters. Minutes later, he set Hailey down on her feet and began to strip completely. He wanted a quick cleansing before lying down with Hailey.

Striding towards the cleanser, he told Hailey, "Go ahead and strip little bird. I will be just a moment and then we can lie down."

Hailey hadn't objected when Jarrek picked her up and carried her towards the room she was staying in with him. That electrical current was running through her body, but she still felt tired. A nap had sounded wonderful. Well, it had sounded wonderful until Jarrek set her on her feet and stripped bare. Both her pussy and mouth began to drool. The way his muscles bunched and shifted as he moved, was so tempting. It was as if all her favorite things rolled into one package, begging her to touch, taste and use him for her pleasure. When he began walking towards the bathroom, his ass flexing and looking so tasty, she had followed along like he was the pied piper.

He stepped into the shower like area and activated the red beams, tilting his head back with his eyes closed. Hailey just stood there and drooled over his body for a few moments, before reaching up to unclasp the pin at her shoulder. Letting her gown pool on the floor she stepped closer.

When the red beams turned white and before Jarrek could open his eyes, she stepped into the cleansing pod with him. Reaching up to run her hands along his chest, she couldn't help but be awed but the contrasts in their skin. She thought that they complimented each other very well, his deep red, hers a light brown with a hint of olive.

Feeling his muscles jump and flex under her fingertips, amazed by how human-like he appeared. If his skin wasn't red, with nipples almost black they were such a dark shade, he could have been mistaken for a native earth resident. She rubbed over his nipples, watching as they drew tight and elongated into a little nub. Leaning up on tiptoes, she licked at his nipples, giving him little bites with her teeth.

She continued, to rub her hands anywhere she could reach. His back, ribs, his flanks and ass. She touched all but the one place she knew he longed for her to touch. Bending down a little, she nibbled her way down his stomach, licking that line of eight pack muscles.

Feeling his hand cup the back of her head and press her tighter to his body, Hailey knew she had him right on the edge of taking over. Trying to keep him there would be the fun part. Finally taking his shaft in her hand, she marveled at the sheer size of it. She couldn't wrap her fingers around the base and he was so long she wondered how she was going to swallow it all. She was willing to find out the answer though. Licking at the head and getting him lubricated with her saliva, Hailey licked up and down the length of his shaft. Squeezing the base of his cock, Hailey danced her hand up and down his shaft in a tight squeeze. Letting the saliva pool in her mouth for a moment, she then opened her mouth and sucked in the head of his cock.

Jarrek's moan reached her ears, making need pool inside her pussy. Setting up a steady rhythm, keeping her hand at the base of his cock, she worked him deeper and deeper into her mouth. The taste of pre-cum had already hit her tongue, assuring her that

Jarrek loved what she was doing to him. Once he reached the back of her throat, she took a deep breath through her nose and swallowed. Feeling his cock pop into her throat, she continued to push Jarrek's cock as deep as it could go. His girth is what stopped her from talking all of him. He was just too wide for her small throat, so Hailey pulled back, took another deep breath and swallowed as much of his cock as she could. Raising her hand from the base, to where she could take him, she set up a steady pace and reveled in his growls of approval and "Yes little bird, swallow my cock.", and "Oh, that feels so good."

Hailey released the grip she had on his cock with her hand, and using all the saliva coating her fingers, used one to breach his back door. Jarrek clenched against her finger once, before allowing her entrance. Probing and finding his prostrate, Hailey used her finger to punch his button in fast strokes, finally causing Jarred to break. He grabbed her hair in a fist with one hand and leaning forward, Jarrek used her hair to hold her in place, while he fucked her mouth in the same rhythm she used to probe his prostrate repeatedly. "Jabir minka!" Jarrek cried. "Swallow me, baby. Take it!" Pushing forward one last time, Jarrek came in a long, plentiful burst. He was salty, spicy, and almost as tasty as his wine. Hailey drank him down and wanted more. Placing a kiss on the head, Hailey straightened and looked up at Jarrek.

Jarrek was blown away. Up to this point, he had initiated all touches or encounters with Hailey. This was the first time she had come to him and he felt honored she was opening up and choosing him. He was also having a hard time coming to grips with how well she had taken his cock. He knew that they were Corduva, but wow. She was perfect.

His heart swelling with the love he had for his beautiful Hailey, Jarrek cupped her face, bent down to place a tender kiss on her lips, and said, "I am so in love with you. You are perfection itself. Come lay with me little bird."

Hailey blinked tears from her eyes, trying not to let Jarrek know how much his words broke her heart. A man could display such tender devotion to a woman when she has just blown his mind with a blowjob or sex. They could almost be poetic.

Unfortunately, that condition rarely lasted past breakfast. More often, it was after a twenty-minute nap. That was okay. Hailey would take what Jarrek offered for the moment; certain she could contain her heartbreak when he changed his mind. He had already given her more than she had received in the past.

She would cherish his passion and tenderness and the uniqueness of this adventure and move on. Letting him snuggle her against his chest, feeling the kiss he placed in her hair, Hailey let sleep claim her.

11.

No Turning Back Now

Hailey was in dream heaven. It started with Jarrek's lips kissing a trail along her spine, his warm male body pressing hers into the mattress, surrounding her in heat and musk, his knee pushing between her legs and spreading her thighs apart. Jarrek's large, warm hand squeezing her hip and pulling her hips up and back. As his long, hot and incredibly hard shaft poked her ass, Hailey pushed back against it.

"Hmm, feels good. Hope the alarm isn't about to go off, ruining the mood and preventing me from finally feeling your cock inside me." Hailey murmured, praying that she was not forced to wake up before she could at least make love to Jarrek here without the consequences of bonding.

"No little bird, nothing will be allowed to interrupt us this time. I just want to make love to you before I go to fight Varill." Jarrek said as he kissed her shoulder and pushed his cock, slowly into the sweetest pussy he had ever felt.

Goddess she was tight. Even though she was wet and he had been arousing her body while she napped, Jarrek could only push his cock inside her in small amounts, as to give her body time to adjust to his size. Her muscles were squeezing him even tighter than his armor had. Once he was fully seated in her warm pussy, Jarrek paused a moment to let her adjust and for him to get a grip on his desires. He wanted to last for Hailey. He wanted to enjoy the feel of her warm, wet depths. Listen to her breathless moans, cries and throaty growls of, "yes, more."

Finally, he was about to experience what no Athrian had experienced in over five thousand years. He was going to be

Corduva to the most beautiful creature the Goddess had ever created. He was trembling. A one thousand four hundred year old hardened warrior, actually trembling at the idea of bonding Hailey. Desire jumbled together with the profound knowledge that he was looking at his people's hope. The possible rebirth of his species. That where one Cordisa was found, many others could be as well.

The soft, silken heat of Hailey pulsed around him and she began to push back against him. Taking the hint that she was ready to feel him move, he slid his cock back out, leaving only the tip, before reversing his thrust and sliding as deep as he could go. Several slow strokes, to assure his self that she was ready; he picked up his pace and moved his hips in different angles, looking for the spots that pleased Hailey the most.

Gritting his teeth against coming before Hailey, he began varying his strokes from the slowest, gentle glide in and out, to really powerful and deep. Using the strokes to learn what Hailey loved the most. He slowed down a little, just enough to spread his legs for better balance and to lean forward and grabbing a pillow, using it to keep her hips tilted at the angle she loved. Using his grip on her hip, he helped tilt her hips up and back even further. This caused Hailey to scream in pleasure, making her pussy to clamp down so hard on his cock, he actually faltered in his stroke for a moment. She held his cock immobile for a heartbeat, before she relaxed enough for him to continue.

Knowing that they were both on the brink of ecstasy, Jarrek put one hand on the mattress next to Hailey's head and one just brushing the side of her breast until he was holding his body just above her in a push-up. Jarrek leaned forward, kissing her shoulders and neck, while continuing to hit the mouth of her womb and listen to her beg and plead for harder, faster, and more. Hailey's pussy began to flutter and contract on his cock and he knew she was about to come.

Lifting his hand from next to her breast, Jarrek brushed Hailey's hair off the nape of her neck. Instead of resting his hand against her breast again, Jarrek cupped her breast and pinched her nipple at the same time he placed a brief kiss to her nape, before he opened his mouth wide and clamped his lips to her neck. Jarrek pushed as deep into her womb as he could when Hailey began screaming her orgasm, and let himself follow her over.

The moment the first jet of his seed entered her body, his symbiot and life's essence pierced Hailey's spinal cord. Releasing half of its self, it traveled up the spinal column, past the medulla to rest in the cerebellum. It would continue to grow over time, but would bond their life forces within hours. Then it would spread throughout the brain learning all of her past and present. Her secrets, fears and dreams once absorbed by the symbiot would then give her all of his hopes, dreams, fears and life experiences, as he absorbed the information from hers. Within a week, they would be in harmony with one another.

Hailey could pinpoint the exact moment she realized she wasn't dreaming about Jarrek making love to her, but that he really was making love to her. The moment he tilted her hips up and hit her bundle of nerves, she knew and screamed. She screamed in part because, damn it felt good. She felt as though the top of her head was going to explode with the pleasure and that electrical current was working triple overtime on her system.

The other reason for her scream was she had just lost the right to choose. Damn vishna! Worse than freaking tequila. When he said it would loosen her inhibitions, she didn't think that meant she would throw herself at him like a broke hooker who found her Pretty Woman moment. She thought it meant that she would feel drunk, want to dance and then strip off her clothes.

Yes, she loved the way he made her feel. She would even admit that deep inside, past her insecurities, she wanted him forever and was thrilled that he had taken the choice away from her. However, that was way down deep and she was nowhere ready to believe he meant forever or that he would always continue to treat her the way he had treated her over the last few days. You just can't fall in love that fast. No matter what people wanted to believe, love happened over time. Lust comes first, and then friendship and love build up over months of working and living side by side. Through laughter, adversity, and even sorrow you got to know a person inside and out. She and Jarrek have had a lot of adversity, even a little sorrow. Where was the laughter, and late night talks? The dinner dates together. Hell, he always woke before her so she didn't even know if he snored or hogged all the covers. How he treated her in front of his men won him a great many points. Even when she was tossing snarky comments and sassing at him, he either didn't get it or thought her sexy.

The way that he worshiped her body was amazing. He had never let her feel as though she were too fat, or that she needed to change anything about herself. Every part of her body had been touched with hands, lips or cock. She flushed a little in remembrance of what he had done to her in the conference room. She had never let anyone back there. Well, to be fair, no one had ever asked, but still. She hadn't given Jarrek a single objection and he had just finished spanking her ass! Even that had felt so wonderful she wanted more. She was squirming all over that table, so turned on she became inarticulate.

Just as she was going to ask Jarrek to stop, no matter how wonderful it all felt, he had changed his position and pinched her nipple, causing her to cry out with the pleasure. Trying to shake that off, long enough for her to get the word stop out, Jarrek had started hitting her g-spot with every single hard thrust.

She couldn't keep from begging for more, he had to keep giving her more, harder and faster. Jarrek had then clamped his mouth down over her neck. All the sensations at once- pinching her nipple, hitting her g-spot and sucking her neck caused her orgasm to throw her into another galaxy.

All she saw were stars, until the pain hit. Something pierced the back of her neck and she knew it was over. No going back, because he had just bonded her to him for life. Thank goodness, the pain was momentary. Hailey almost wanted to laugh, except she also wanted to cry. She would have to catch her breath, before she could do both. It might be worth it if she kept getting such wonderful sex, but she never made that choice for herself. Only time would tell if they would make it.

Jarrek gently pulled from his beloved's body. He was not ready to leave the tight warm haven, but wanted to hold his mate in his arms while he caught his breath. He stretched out next to Hailey and then pulled her body over his chest. Letting her head lay against the heart that beat for her and their daughter. "My love. My little bird. My Cordisa Inca." Kissing her hair and stroking his fingers up and down her spine. When Hailey lifted her head up to him and glared, with fire in her eyes, Jarrek paused and asked, "What is wrong my beloved?"

Hailey pushed against his chest and rolled out of his hold, pulling the crumbled sheets and using it to cover her body from his gaze. Pushing the hair out of her face, she told him exactly what was wrong.

"How can you ask what is wrong? You bonded me without my permission! You explained nothing of this process to me. I had to ask Sidhawk about it. I have told you repeatedly, that I am not your Cordisa and want to be taken back home. Do you care or consider my feelings? No. You did what you wanted. So like a man, dammit." Hailey took a breath to calm down a little. She didn't know why she even bothered. Sidhawk made it seem like a forever deal. Jarrek started to speak up and she held her hand up for him to stop.

"Look. I am sorry. I like you Jarrek. You do things to my body and treat me like a goddess, but I don't know you. We haven't spent any real time together, just talking and learning about each other. I can't and won't be with someone who cannot consider my wants. I have been down that path and it leads to heartache and depression. Is there a way to undo the bond? I never got to ask."

Jarrek felt as though she was shredding his soul with her words. The happiest moment of his, life and it had just been broken into a billion pieces. Tears rushed to his eyes, but he did his best to push them back as he said in a voice made gravelly from the suppressed emotions, "You hate me so much, little bird? I thought that you had chosen me when you followed me into the cleanser and initiated our love play. I thought you were as happy as I am that we had found one another in the googolplexes of stars and planets in the galaxies. I am sorry that you do not find that I am good enough for you, but there is no way to undo the bond that is known to me."

Jarrek stood up from the bed and straightened his shoulders. Going to the wall he dialed up another suit of armor; dressing he turned to her and gave a small bow and said, "I apologize Hailey, but I must attend to my duties at this time. I am neglecting my people. I will give you your space and will see if there is something that I can do to give you your freedom from me and dissolve our bond."

Jarrek turned and strode from the room as fast as possible. He did not wish to unman himself by falling to his knees crying and begging her to love him as much as he loved her. Mayhap Loku could counsel him on where he had gone wrong. If there was anyone on this ship who knew everything about him, it would be his friend from boyhood and former lover. He also would not expect him to hold back the tears that were threatening to fall even now.

Hailey watched Jarrek leave and didn't miss the significance of his calling her by name. He rarely even used it. Preferring to call her Jabir minka or my little bird, which meant the same thing, but one she heard in English and the other in his language. It seemed to depend on how he said it to her. Hailey saw the stiffness in his gait when he walked out the door and hated that she had upset him. He would recover with time.

She knew that to most men, women were as interchangeable as batteries. He would find another woman that he could worship with his lips and hands and body. She ignored the fact that the idea of him with another woman squeezed her heart in a vise and made jealousy raise its big ugly head, curl her hands into fists for the fight and snarl a challenge.

Her heart already saw them as a couple. Her soul felt whole and complete when in his arms and presence, but too many times she had followed her heart and been crushed into the dirt. It was why she waited with Greg. Waiting until he proposed before she lowered her guard, and look how that ended. She had almost killed herself. She hadn't even told her momma just how close she had come.

If she could get the bond to break before it took hold, then she could escape before she gave any more of herself to Jarrek. If the bond couldn't be severed and Jarrek changed his mind, started asking her to lose weight or started criticizing her, than that would be the end of her. She would give in and just end it. He really had to find a way break it soon.

Hailey got out bed and went to the cleanup. Jarrek needed time away from her, she understood, but she wouldn't be stuck in this room while everyone else was working at something. There had to be something she could do. Finding her gown on the floor just inside the bathroom, she put it back on and stepped into the energy shower. She didn't know how to make another, so she hoped it would work on her gown as well.

Three minutes later, she was stepping out of Jarrek's room and walking down the corridor towards the elevator. Just as she was about to step inside she heard her name called. Turning around she was pleased to see Sidhawk and another man coming towards her.

"Hey Sid. I'm glad you found me. I was hoping to find something to do or someway to help contribute to the battle about to take place." Hailey said.

"You wish to contribute? This is good. Let us go back to Jarrek's rooms so that I may converse with you. I have an idea on how you can help." The stranger said to her.

"Um sure. Who are you? Have we met?" Hailey asked. He looked pissed at her, but she had never met him before. She looked at him closely trying to see if she had seen him somewhere on the ship. He would be handsome if he wasn't looking so angry.

He was taller even than Jarrek by about four inches with the deepest brown hair she had ever seen. With its black highlights it almost turned it all black. His skin was the same deep red of Jarrek's but he had obsidian and gold eyes. His mouth was pinched in anger so she didn't know how full his lips were, but he had a square jaw and hawk-like nose.

He was just a muscular as Jarrek, but looked even more dangerous. She wasn't sure she wanted to be alone with him. "Only if Sidhawk is present. I have not been introduced to you. I know Jarrek said that I was safe here, but I would rather not take that chance. I'm sure you understand."

"My name, if you require it, is Loku Rai Trindon. I am the Senior First Officer of this battle destroyer. I am also Jarrek's best friend. I have been his companion since we were four ansis old. I will not harm you. To harm you would be to harm Jarrek and that is something that I would die before I do. This is something that you, apparently, do not know the meaning of, or feel. Now, let us go to your rooms." Loku told her and began to lead her back the way she came.

Hailey pulled her arm from Loku's grip and stepped back. "I don't think so. If you have something, you wish to say to me, that's fine. You can say it right here and right now and then go back to your duties, or just piss off."

Loku looked down at the gorgeous woman in front of him and felt nothing but disgust. She held the soul of a man who would die for her, and she looked as though she did not care. She just took it and tore it, crushed it and then ground it under her dainty feet.

"Fine. I do not care if others hear. I was only trying to show you a common courtesy. Another thing you seem to be lacking. Yes, you are gorgeous, beyond compare, I freely admit it, but your outer beauty is only that, outer. You must be heartless and without a soul if you can treat my Prince in the manner that you have. This man sings your praises to all. Talks endlessly of your beauty, how much he loves you and what he wants to show you, or give you when we get back to our native planet. I am sick of hearing how much he desires you, but that he is scared that you won't be able to handle his passion, as you are a delicate blossom that he doesn't want to crush. You want to contribute and help this battle, well then you can take your tiny ass up to the bridge, get on your knees, and then apologize to Jarrek. I understand that you are his Cordisa and due some modicum of respect, but respect must be earned, and you have not earned mine. He is thinking of giving himself to Varill so that he can die and you can be free. You took the most precious moment of his life and turned it into something worse than his greatest nightmare. Now, he contemplates leaving our world without its next leader. Why, because he bonded your lives together and he did not, what? Did he forget to declare his undying love for you to all? Perhaps he forgot to make some grand gesture. Has he not shown you with every atom and molecule of his being that he will love you for all time? Please tell me."

Inside Hailey was crying at the horrible words coming out of Loku's mouth. Outside all she showed was pissed. "I must say that it sure is real nice to meet someone who is omnipotent. So omnipotent, that he knows of the horrors of my life and past. Knows of the things that remain buried deep and have never seen the light of day to anyone other than my nightmares, and yet, still sees me as heartless for wanting a choice. For wanting time to speak with Jarrek and find out who he is, what he stands for, believes in. That I am at fault for wanting some say in how my life is to be. I am sorry that I have broken his heart. I feel as though he did the same to me when he did not ask if I was ready to bond." Hailey spewed angrily at Loku, embarrassed to feel a few tears slip from the hold she was trying to keep on them and slide down her cheek. Swiping at them impatiently, she told Loku.

"Instead of standing here chastising me for something that is clearly not your business, why don't you tell him how much better he is without me and help him find a way to break the bond without his death? I may be the evil bitch as far as you are concerned, but I care for Jarrek very much and would never want to see him dead. Now, unless your jealousy has more to impart, fuck off." Not actually giving Loku a chance to spew any more vitriol her way, Hailey stepped around him and walked off down the corridor. She would find somewhere else to be.

12.

Conversation with a Goddess

Sidhawk looked over at Loku and contemplated hitting him. He was so angry that Loku had dragged him to witness that conversation. "I cannot believe that you forced me to witness that. What is wrong with you?" He asked.

"What? You know why I am angry. She told Jarrek that she wants him to find a way to undo the bond. She has rejected him. You know what this means to him, to all of us." Loku answered. Completely taken by surprise with the amount of anger Sidhawk was showing him. The little engineer was normally the most placid of individuals. Rarely angry, he was submissive to Kirrek's wants and desires.

"She was right, you know. We know nothing of her life. From the little bit of information gleamed from our conversations, she led me to believe that the men of her planet think her fat and undesirable. Now she finds herself in a situation that is the opposite and Jarrek has worshiped her. She would find that suspicious, in truth, so would you find it. I would if our positions reversed. Add to that the discovery of what the Krakill did to her body; something she was unaware of until that message came through. She then watched, as her body is debased, abused and violated. Not only to see, but know that a portion of the crew saw her in that position, would you want someone to see that happen to you? Take just that small bit into account, the small part of her life that we are aware. Would you be ready to jump headfirst into a relationship because someone said to you that it was fated? Theirs to love protect and bond? Jarrek is so in love with her that he considers what went on before he found her inconsequential; he has not necessarily dismissed those concerns, but knows that he can remedy them through their bond. She is not from our planet and they do not bond on her world. They only have a ceremony to join as a couple. Jarrek had not explained the bonding to her. I did when she asked and I know that I probably did a poor job of it. Tell me true Loku, would you then wish to bond? Would you not wish to return to what is familiar and known to you? No matter that, things are not ideal and you are unhappy?"

"Shivak loch croin! You know the answer to that already Sidhawk. I am a Cruvek and know it. I did not stop to think when Jarrek all but said that he was going to die to free her. I panicked and wanted to make her apologize and make him happy. He cannot die. Do the males of her planet really think that she is undesirable? The whole male population must be stupid." Loku felt horrible now. Sidhawk had made him think of the situation from her perspective and he liked it not at all. He needed to return to Jarrek and convince him that not all was lost. To make the same points to Jarrek that Sidhawk had made to him. "I am off to try to convince our Prince that all is not lost. Say a prayer to the Goddess that this all turns out right. When it is, I will apologize to our Queen on my knees and offer her my head. Think you that will be enough?" Loku asked.

"I personally think that when Jarrek absorbs that memory, you will require more mercy from him. Good luck." Sidhawk offered before taking off in the direction Hailey went.

Hailey had no clue where she was at, or where she was going. Ever since her abduction, all these stupid girly feelings were everywhere. She had cried more during this episode in her life, than ever. Even during her teenage crush years, she hadn't been this bad. Edmondson women, didn't cry, they got things done and cried in private. Yet, she had cried on Jarrek several times now and then in front of that big jerk. He was just jealous that he would need to find a new sex partner if they couldn't break the bond.

Turning a corner she found herself in a front of a jewel encrusted door. Stepping forward the doors parted and Hailey sucked in her breath. She found herself in a beautiful atrium filled with flowers and growing plant life. The ceiling was at least fifty feet high and was covered in stars. Hailey wasn't sure if it was a fresco painting or real stars it was so amazing. Continuing forward slowly, she ran her fingers over leaves, petals, and stamens. She leaned forward to see what they all smelled like. Each was unique, but blended together to perfume the air in an intoxicating bouquet. This place was gorgeous. She could spend hours in this room.

Hailey came to a columned archway with white velvet curtains tied open to reveal a garden and a statue of a woman who was curvy and as generously proportioned as she was. She could have been gazing at herself in the mirror, with the exception of facial features and hair. The only word that came to mind was, "Wow." This was surely their chapel. Sidhawk had mentioned they worshiped the Goddess.

She stood proudly, with her shoulders
back, her breasts pushed out to tempt a man.
She had one hip cocked and the gown they
had put her in, wrapped around her neck and
crisscrossed her breasts tightly enough to
show protruding nipples. It wrapped around
her hip and pinned together at the joint
there, with a small rope chain. Leaving the
right side gaping and showing all of the right
leg and ending at the left ankle. Her right
arm was cocked on her right hip above the
chain and her left hand was outstretched as
if to greet a lover. Her expression shouted
sexy, passion filled nights.

A curving bench in a semi-circle sat
in front of the Goddess with pillowed
cushions. At her feet were thousands upon
thousands of letters. Some sealed, some
open to anyone's perusal. Hailey walked up
to the statue and ran a hand over the
Goddesses outstretched hand.

"So you are the Goddess, huh? They
never told me your name. Wonder if they
consider your name sacred, so don't use it
often. Well, I'm in a fix all right. Jarrek
insists we are fated hearts, that you created

us to be together, but where I come from, that kind of thing doesn't exist. Well, some people believe in soul mates. I used to be one of them. A secret romantic, covered in snark and sass and destined to be hurt repeatedly until I threw in the towel and became a realist. I'm not sure I want to be bonded. I had Sidhawk describe it to me, ya know? Talk about scary! That is what a real horror story looks like to me. My planet delights in trying to tell stories that scare you and make you scream. Too bad I always either laughed so hard I almost peed my pants, or rolled my eyes because the storyline was ridiculous. All they really needed was the idea of bonding. To have no secrets allowed between mates, nowhere to hide the nightmares, every thought, feeling and experience to lay bare before another? That scares every cell in my body. You really should have thought about that a little more, my friend. No one really wants to know the truth of your thoughts. They want banalities, and for you to agree with the way they feel and think. Sometimes, all someone needs is just a body to listen." Hailey finished tracing the statues hand and stepped away to recline on the bench. Just as she had reclined completely, she almost did scream. The statue lowered her arm and stepped towards her. "Holy crap!" Hailey cried and moved to roll off the bench and run away when the statue spoke to her.

"Darling there is nothing holy about crap. It's just shit. We all must on occasion. Now please don't have a heart attack dear, as I must be brief. Yes, I am really talking with you. . I am Annikatalamenaria. You may call me Annika or Goddess. I have animated this statue for a brief moment so that I can try to smack some sense into your southern head. Yes, I know who you are and your life story. Can we skip the disbelief section and go right to the Jarrek is your mate section and move on? Thank you. Yes, my daughter, I made Jarrek just for you. I am sorry that your life was toughI am sorry for Greg and all the other idiots. Some were destined and some were unfortunately life on your planet. You reached a little closer to the edge than I liked, so I sent your mother to help pull you away from it. I loved your snark to Loku. He needs more of it and just waits until he sees whom I have destined for him! Girl you are going to laugh so hard you pee!'"

Annika slapped her knee lightly at that, and sat down next to her. She put on a serious face and said, "However, you made some good points that I don't think that you realize should have also applied to you. Did you stop to think, what Jarrek was feeling or going through? He has been waiting for fourteen hundred years for the gift that you are to him. You have waited a measly, well we won't discuss age. It's rude between women. He knew what a bond entailed, grew up praying to me about it. Looked forward to a day when he could meet and love you with everything that he is, even if he had to cross over to the other side without finding you here while he was alive. As soon as his body let him know that *you* were that promise, he loved you. Jarrek will take all that has happened in your past, every horror visited upon you and they will be as nothing to him. They will be something to avenge, another excuse to hold you and love your body to replace those horrible things. To share the burden until it is as light as a feather and easily discarded. That my dear is a bond. You will know, with every fiber of your being that he loves you, lives for you and will lay a universe at your feet if you need it. He thought you had decided to accept him as you came to him in the cleanser. He didn't stop to think of the vishna and the affect it had on you, even though he was warned of the possible side effects. He was elated to be able to bond you and spend his life loving you. By the way, vishna is ten times worse than tequila dear. It will wipe away all you inhibitions. Quite delicious stuff, I know. I pop over to Jarrek's estate whenever I need another case."

Leaning forward towards Hailey, Annika continued. "Look sweetie, I don't have a lot of time left to chat. I have a golf date with Lucifer and need to get the girly parts ready to distract the sorry bastard," she said as she plumped her breasts and had them bouncing. "He will cheat if you don't keep a sharp eye; or keep his eyes occupied on something else." Annika gave a little laugh and stood up, walking over to the statue's pedestal. "Now, there is no way to break the bond unless I break it and I will tell you right now to forget it. He is perfect for you dear and you are the answer to all of his dreams and wishes. Would you like to see? Here is one from about a year ago." The letter floated to her on an invisible breeze. Oh, and Hailey. Read fast my dear. Your lover is about to try to get himself killed to give you your freedom. He blew off Loku, and took the team to rescue your daughter and Kirrek. You need to make your choice soon, before it is too late and he succeeds in giving you a wish that you really don't want. Don't forget that I know your heart." With a final blown kiss in her direction, she stepped onto the pedestal and turned back into a statue.

Looking down at the letter in her hand, she wondered if she should even bother to read it. If she wasn't actually losing her mind, and in a psychiatric institution right now on some really good drugs, and somehow she just didn't think her imagination that good, than a real live Goddess had just told her all she needed to know. Making up her mind, she tucked the letter into the top of her gown and got to her feet. She needed to find Loku or Sidhawk and figure out how to use this bond to save her mates ass.

How could she let him know she loved him and have some wonderful make up sex if he wasn't here for them to start? She was still going to demand to go home, but only to kidnap momma. She was not going to be Queen of a planet she had never dreamed existed or be a momma to her own daughter without her own to help give her advice when she was being an idiot.

Her momma would have been able to do what the Goddess just did for her, but she would have smacked her upside the head about two days ago. "Thanks for the pep talk Annika. Look out, my Corduva; I'm coming to save your ass."

13.

Rescue

Inside the new stealth prototype that Bruthus had designed, Jarrek was miserable. He kept trying to concentrate on what he needed to accomplish. Kill Varill, so that his daughter and Cordisa were safe and never had to worry for their lives. Save his stupid brother if time permitted. When Kirrek recovered, he was going to kick his ass and put him back under medical care. How many times, has he had to pull his ass from a bad situation? He would need to grow up and lead their people when Varill killed him. Well, if Varill killed him. He may need to do the deed himself. Krakill's were so stupid that unless he helped pull the trigger himself, he would have grown bored with the torture they liked to dish out first and just kill everyone.

Varill did possess one thing in abundance though. Luck. He had been trying for the last one hundred years to kill the shivak loch croin and had come very close, but he somehow managed to escape. The last time he had tried to kill Varill, he had taken some merchants word that Varill was on a certain ship and the idiot had mixed the name with the ship next to him. Jarrek had taught him the error of his ways on that one for sure. He wanted no mistakes this time.

"We follow the earlier plan we came up with. Marthos, when you finish helping Sameth secure my daughter; I want you to scout around very quickly to make sure that there is no way Varill could escape this time. Disable all escape vehicles, pods or shuttles you run across. Rometho has about two hundred button explosives that are small, but very effective. He showed me the simulation of the explosive and I was quite impressed. Toss a button inside a pod and when detonated, destroyed. When the flash dies down there is barely any debris left; it is the same for a small to medium sized vehicle. Two buttons are required for larger vehicles like individual attack ships. Three for a large escape shuttle similar to the ones we have on board the Sh'dow al D'th. Remember that we have no more than an hour before the game is up and they discover either that Kirrek or my daughter is missing. Quick, quiet and covert are our bywords for this mission." He heard Rometho tell Marthos where to locate the button explosives he would need.

Bruthus spoke up from the front seat, "Docking with target in two verls, Commander."

Jarrek stood and went to the front of the shuttle; turning he spoke to his men. "All right Warriors. I count on all of you to help in keeping my Cordisa and daughter safe. Stay the course, concentrate on your targets and once completed, feel free to kill as many as you can. Remember, that your kills cannot be discovered right away though, so prudence is required. If we fail, we fail our entire planet. I do not wish for my name to be so besmirched. Do you?" Jarrek asked and when his warriors screamed their denial, continued. "Go with the Goddess. Conquer the enemy and fight with cunning and ruthlessness." They all screamed out their battle cry and waited the last minute that Bruthus called out.

Jarrek stopped at Marthos and sat next to him. "Cousin, I charge you with this task. If I fall, I require that you make sure that my brother and daughter are returned to the ship safely and that you speed with all haste to my father, so that they can make sure my daughter and Cordisa are protected and loved. Kirrek is to assume my leadership role for our planet until such time that my daughter can grow up to take his place as my heir. He is no longer allowed on missions, but instead he is to make sure that my daughter is guarded and groomed to rule our planet. How say you?" Jarrek asked in the voice he used as the Prince and next ruler of their planet.

"My Prince, I accept your task and will see it through, but tells you that you are stupid if you think that the Krakill's could actually kill you." Marthos took his responsibility to Athria very seriously, but could not help but laugh at the suggestion that Varill could succeed in killing his Prince. He had been trying for over a hundred years and had not managed yet. While Varill kept to the tactics that his race had used for a millennium, they had improved theirs at every opportunity. Like the ship they were in, and the new explosives that Rometho had generated, they practically guaranteed their own victory.

"Warrior Barion, when a man goes to battle, he does so with the expectation that he may go to greet the Goddess and prepares. That those left behind are taken care of, and know that they were the most important thing in your world all the way to the end. No battle goes the way you wish. Otherwise we would have no need of warriors, if we could just wish the outcome we desire." Jarrek counseled his young cousin. With that statement, Marthos was showing his youth. He was a great sniper, but hardly battle tested like his other warriors.

"I apologize, Sire. You are correct. Now that a Cordisa has been found, we can begin to think to the future and make sure they are at the forefront of all plans and contingencies." Marthos said solemnly, giving his Prince a small bow with his hand over his heart.

Jarrek never felt the shuttle dock with Varill's ship; it was so smooth, sending a quick compliment and a hearty smack on the back when Bruthus stood with the others, ready to begin their plans. "All right, everyone check your comms quickly." Jarrek ordered. Once everyone was signaling that they were online, he sent Marthos ahead to get the way clear and cover them in the case of discovery.

"Click your comms twice to signal when you have completed your mission." All the men signaled their acknowledgment, received the all clear from Marthos, disembarked and began to carry out their individual assignments.

Jarrek was proud of his Warriors and sent a prayer to the Goddess that they were successful. He gave his men twenty minutes before he made his way out of the ship to hunt for Varill. He would be the one to kill him if at all possible. Slipping between fighter ships, and other scout ships, he was angry with himself for not grabbing a handful of Rometho's button bombs. He must clear his head and focus on killing Varill, instead of his misery. If he did not focus, he would die before he could find Varill or be assured that his men had laid all the bombs required to blow Varill into hell.

Jarrek paused briefly outside the door of the ship's interior. He heard a double click in his headset and smiled. One mission completed, two more to go. Moving double time he moved as fast as possible through the boring gray of the ships interior. All of the Krakill's ships were the same. This of course was quite a boon for him, as by now every warrior on his planet could maneuver through the corridors blindfolded, but the stench had never been something they could ever become accustomed to.

His little bird named them correctly. His chest squeezed painfully at the thought of his little bird. He had been thinking non-stop of what she said to him. He finally remembered how much vishna Hailey had consumed, and what effect it had on her. She was right; he had not asked or considered all that she had been through since their meeting. Was is not just mere days ago he had shown her the video sent of what had been done to her? He would not wish to bond if that had just happened to him. He had kicked himself repeatedly over the last twenty hours since he had left her.

This was the first mission Sameth had been on with his younger brother since he had joined the ship on their last docking at home. Sameth was startled by the difference in his bothers demeanor, and tried to speak about it, but Marthos put him off at each occasion. Now was not the time as he followed Marthos down the twisting corridors, to their medical and genetic wards.

Watching as Marthos moved like a zilenta, stalking and quiet. He paused to give the signal for patrols headed their direction and they each took a door and as quietly as possible gave a quick glance inside and then hid just inside the door. Letting the small group pass them, they continued on their way. Turning left at the next corridor Marthos ran into a lone Krakill scientist. Quickly covering the startled scientist's mouth, he pulled his knife and slit his throat with the other. The blue blood splashed Marthos face and arms.

Sameth hurried over and grabbed his legs, helping to carry him to one of the open rooms they had just left. Stuffing the body in a closet and taking the uniforms hanging there to lie atop the body and soak up the blood. No use in hiding the body, if they were going to leave a pool of blood back to the evidence.

Marthos wiped his face and hands and they continued as silent as ever. Two corridors later, they were just outside of their medical lab. Hand signals letting Sameth know exactly what Marthos planned, Sameth found himself boosting his brother into an air vent that ran parallel. Moving back a little, Sameth looked for a side closet to wait out Marthos' scouting, and found an electrical closet. Keeping the door open a sliver, watching for the first sign Marthos had returned with their object's location.

Six minutes later, he was beginning to worry. It should not have taken him this long to locate one embryo bearing Athrian heritage in their files. A small, barely discernible tweet on the air caused the breath to leave his body. He had found her. Rushing to catch up to his brother, he saw his arm hanging down from the vent shaft. Standing under the vent, he looked up at his brother questioningly. Three hand signals later, he reached up for his brother's hand and jumped as he pulled him into the vent with him. "This way." Marthos whispered.

Pushing himself backward until he could turn around he led Sameth to the lab housing six scientists and a two foot by two foot canister housing a pink fluid and a rapidly growing Athrian child. Noting where each warrior stood, they divided the kills between them and then bursting through the vent went into action. He watched Marthos fall through the vent; land on his feet and one large step put him behind his first victim. Slamming his blade into his enemy's back and angled up to pierce the lung and heart, allowing a fast, quiet kill. The Krakill never had time to turn around.

Sameth quickly followed, but as he had a longer sword strapped to his back had to wait until he landed on his feet to pull the blade. He sent it in a quick arc around his head and felt as it sliced cleanly though one of his opponent's head, severing it from the body. Stepping to the left to avoid the fall of the body that did not quite realize it was dead; he stabbed upward through the next body, right through the heart and out the spine. Pulling the blade free in another dancing move to the side, this time to the right, he dispatched his next opponent.

His last opponent was about to push the alarm, so he quickly cut off the reaching arm and before he could scream his denial, had sliced his head in two pieces. Reaching over the last body, Sameth grabbed a cloth and wiped the blood from his blade. Returning it to his sheath he turned and stepped around the blood and bodies Marthos was beginning to move under the table, while simultaneously wiping up blood with towels he dragged under his feet.

Reading the information, they had gathered on the first female Athrian in close to six thousand years, he copied the data and then deleted as he went until nothing remained on their systems. Whether they blew up the ship or not; nothing would survive to tell the tale, they had created one of their women. Once finished he quickly searched for Hailey's information, and copied and deleted it as well. The Krakill's never needed to know about the fertile planet they found, or their new Queen.

He did a quick search of any other information the Krakill had on their race, finding something so shocking, he almost forgot they were on a timer. He copied the information, and deleted it from their hard drives. He hoped they were able to blow this entire ship into dust.

He unhooked the baby's systems, transferring them over to a portable pack one system at a time, so as not to stress the baby. When he had completed his task, he found Marthos ready to depart and he helped him back up into the vent. Handing him the precious female child as carefully as possible, he waited for Marthos to get her situated and place his arm out to help him back up.

The return was a little slower as they could only go so far before they needed to bring the baby carefully forward. When they found themselves outside the vent where they had entered, they found that they would need to wait until a contingent of warriors could enter the section with three large eggs on a trolley. Sameth briefly wondered if that was Hailey's children being rolled by, but quickly pushed the thought away. It did not make a difference if they were; according to Sidhawk, there was no way he could save them, yet he paused briefly to mourn the passing of innocents.

Once out of the vent, he waited for Marthos to hand the baby down to him and jumps down. Marthos would take point and do any fighting that was needed while he carried the Princess. He would only intervene if it looked like Marthos was outnumbered or the enemy was about to sound the alarm. They were lucky on the return trip as it went very smoothly. There was one guard outside the launch bay, but he was easily dispatched and hidden.

They were back on board with their Princess securely strapped in and feeding off their electrical systems instead of the portable, so Marthos double clicked their completion and left to begin his next task. Throwing button bombs into all the vehicles and pods out there, while he guarded the baby and waited to start healing Kirrek as soon as the twins returned from rescuing him. Well versed in Krakill torture and Kirrek in particular, he was ready the sec they brought him on board. He sent a prayer to the Goddess that they were having no trouble. He also needed to relay to his commander what he had found.

Heathrick and Shemrick glided along the corridors towards the back of the ship where Jarrek and his team had just escaped. They were not worried about being spotted, as they used their energy as a field around their bodies to bend light and refract back the corridor around them. In effect making them invisible. They had discovered this unique ability by chance while they were children. They had been hiding from their papa, who was bent on tanning their backside for accidentally burning the barn down.

Just as they were trembling in anticipation, for the pain of the strapping they were about to get, certain they were now caught, their poppa had walked right by them. Of course they still got the strapping, but not until later when they went into the house for evening meal, and were snatched by the ear and dragged to the punishment room. They had not found any other warriors or twins who could do the same thing, and had been unsuccessful on teaching others how to.

They did worry that they actually saw no warriors or personnel as they walked the corridors. Something was suspicious. Right before the large cargo area of cages and slave pens, a miniature cargo bay resided. Ten torture rooms, five on each side, made up this must-visit spot on the ship. A must visit spot, as traditionally, Krakill's loved torture. The screams actually got them horny. It helped them produce the necessary chemicals to lay their egg for fertilizing. Sick, right? Sick was seeing them get hard from breaking your bones or cutting into your body, as they knew first hand. It had happened only once, but they gave a brief shudder as they stepped into an Athrian's hell.

Splitting up they each looked inside the small window. Shemrick found one of the warriors who had gone along with Kirrek dead in the first cell he looked in. Quickly stepping inside he wrapped the body in Shashay and pushed a small button on the side. This reduced the warrior to ash and shrunk down to a pouch that he tucked into a pocket on his vest. Continuing his search, Shemrick found Kirrek alive in the next cell and signaled his brother with a short, low whistle. Kirrek looked in bad shape.

Heathrick quickly searched the other windows for occupants, and found something so horrible he let out a low curse. Surprised, Shemrick went over to see what was wrong and sucked in his breath it was so bad.

Whereas Kirrek had been beaten and cut up, this small female had been beaten and carved up and parts of her skin were missing on her breasts, thighs and belly. She was hanging naked, suspended from chains and her own body was killing her slowly. Her body had pulled away from the wall in her exhaustion, her strength had given out and she could no longer keep it upright, causing her arms to be wrenched out of the sockets from her own weight. Her head was slumped forward, the chained collar around her neck cutting off her oxygen, choking her. She would be dead soon if they did not intervene. Heathrick nodded to Shemrick's unasked question, and quickly went inside to release her.

Heathrick was careful to tilt her head back and fold her arms against her breasts. She was so close to death she did not even scream when he released her, or when he folded her arms in front of her. Carefully picking her up as though she was a child, he made sure to carry her tight against his chest. Shemrick went to Kirrek and threw him over his shoulder.

They quickly returned to the shuttle so that Sameth could work on the little human they had found. She would need Sameth a whole lot more than Kirrek. They gave the completion signal right as they stepped onto the ship and closed the doors. They bellowed for Sameth as soon as it became safe to do so, while walking back to the medical compartment set aside for this trip. They both sent a prayer to the Goddess that she would survive while they continued towards Sameth. They had not found the other warrior said to have been with Kirrek, and could only pray for his soul if he was unrecoverable.

Another double click sounded in his ear and brought Jarrek back to the mission at hand. One mission left. Time to get busy. Jarrek paused at end of the corridor, trying to listen for conversation or movement. He wanted to find out which missions had been completed, but did not want to risk speaking in a voice that would carry and get him caught. It was enough to know that his men had succeeded at their missions. Jarrek heard no movement or conversation, so stepped around the corner and continued.

He did not like the feeling in his gut that warned something was wrong. Where were the personnel? Where were the warriors? Where they off trying to sneak aboard his ship? It was not one of their normal tactics, but something was off, and he could not think of what it could be. Had Varill killed off most of his crew? Since they could manipulate DNA and base pairs, they usually had contingents of warriors frozen to replace any that were killed for stupidity or in battle. This ship almost echoed its state of emptiness. Goddess willing, perhaps they were succeeding in killing them off. He would have to ask Varill, right before he killed him.

Stopping at another corridor, he again paused to listen for movement or conversation and this time heard something moving away from him talking. Peaking his head around the corridor, he watched as two Krakill drug the body of one of his warriors. Looks like they had tortured him away from their usual spot. Why? He could not make out what they were saying, so he began following behind them. He watched to see where they would take him. He hoped that he could rescue his warrior before continuing his mission. He wished he could tell who the warrior was, but from this distance, and his head almost touching the ground was unable to see his face. He watched them drag his warrior into a room along the corridor.

Trying to hurry to the door so he could hear any conversation between them and find out what was going on. What he did hear caused his anger to spike. One Krakill, bitching to the other to hurry up, so he could have a turn made him wonder of what they spoke. Torture? They usually traded off anyway, so what was he speaking of?

Then Jarrek heard, "Shut it. I found the vid, Krukick. I get to go first. You can have the front like I showed you, then we can trade places and you can shove your rod inside his hole. It looked fun and the squishy human in the vid looked as though it was painful and horrifying. Got my rod hard just watching. We can keep him all to ourselves now. I will go back and put in that he died of his wounds and we can do whatever we want with him for as long as he stays alive."

His horror growing with each word, Jarrek felt his fury rise. They were talking about raping one of his warriors! Not while he still lived. Hearing his warrior begin to scream and then have it muffled, he knew that they were starting. Well, they would not get much farther. Unsheathing both of his swords, he pushed the activation button with the back of one hand tightfisted around his sword, and went in swinging. They were dead before they knew he had even interrupted them. Too bad. They did not deserve the quick death he gave them.

Going to the table, he touched his warriors exposed shoulder, ducking at the slow fist thrown his way. "'Tis fine warrior, you are free now. How badly are you injured?" Jarrek asked in a voice devoid of emotion. Warriors may give one another relief, but never by force. It was a quick way to get sentenced to death. He would not treat his warrior with anything other than respect, nor remark on what was done. It was for his partner of choice to help him work through any issues that arose.

Jarrek saw no shame in what had been forced upon him. They were dead, and he was avenged. "Your captors are dead on the floor. We need to get out of here before we become discovered. Now I ask you again warrior, how badly are you injured?" Jarrek asked a little more forcefully.

Darthos S'et Valleyark finally heard the question put to him and raised his head. Finding his Commander and Prince standing over him confused him for a moment, while the last several days replayed in his head. Once the replay had finished, he almost whimpered. Struggling to stand and cover himself, he replied, "I am not hurt too badly Commander. They have been working on Cloge the most. I think that they killed him early this morning, as they then came to me with more frequency. The beatings and cuttings are not too bad. I am not new to that torture of theirs. The rapes are something new though. Cloge warned me it was coming. He unfortunately had many visitors hurt him. They have discovered some kind of entertainment vids from the marble planet that has gotten them salivating and curious. Between Cloge, the female, and me I think that they must have all had a turn, until these two grabbed me. Varill's second in command really likes the female, poor woman. I wish that I could have saved her. The screams were worse than anything they did to me. Domu! They have discovered a way to prevent our morph Commander. We must find out how they did it and destroy that information."

The urgency of that last bit of information made Darthos want to kick himself. He should have started with that first. Unfortunately, he was a little confused from the starvation and dehydration. He was able to redress without the help of his Commanding officer, thank the Goddess, but they needed to find where that information was kept and retrieve it. Now ready, he took the sword that Prince Jarrek held out to him and prayed that he would be able to use it. His body hurt and protested moving. He would never shame himself in front of his Commander and Prince by admitting he was not ready to defend himself.

Jarrek looked at Darthos' stance and could see the pain he was in. Not needing him to kill Varill, he turned to his warrior and said, "I am off to kill Varill. I have teams rescuing my brother and daughter and placing bombs throughout the ship. I am sure they will find Cloge's body and the female if she is still alive. All that I require of you at this time is that you return to the ship and tell Heathrick and Shemrick of your discovery. Perhaps they can find where this information is located and retrieve it before the bombs are set. If not, it will not be a problem for long. We are going to make this ship disappear into little dust motes. No trace will remain to lead others of their race to this sector of space. I know Varill is a greedy cruvek and will not have shared this information with anyone outside this ship. Only if his entire ship and life were about to be exterminated would he bother to share. Then, only because his genetic make-up demands it. So hurry to the launch bay. At the farthest corner in the west, there is one pod and two fighter jets set for repairs. Take this to uncloak Bruthus' new ship, and open the doors." Handing Darthos the re-cloaking device, Jarrek left him to carry out his orders.

He could feel the time slipping through his hands and needed to get this finished. He had fifteen minutes left at the most before they discovered the rescue mission and started searching the ship for them and firing on his own. Before the laser cannons started firing he needed to be sure that his team was safely aboard his ship and headed towards Athria with all speed. If only a few of his other battle destroyers could arrive in this sector of space. That would make Mr. Stinky, as his beloved called Varill, pause and retreat. The third double-click sounded in his ear. All the bombs were in place and both his brother and daughter were safe in his people's possession. Hopefully, they had rescued the other woman that Darthos was talking about.

Jarrek sent a prayer to the Goddess, that when he joined her she would allow him the boon of watching over his Cordisa and daughter. If he could not be with them in life, then he wanted to protect them in death.

Getting closer to Varill and the bridge, Jarrek still worried over the fact that he was having too easy a time. Just running into two Krakill while heading to the bridge was wrong. By this time on any other mission he had laid between ten to twenty down. This felt wrong. Taking the advice of his gut, Jarrek peeled off the corridor to enter the first unoccupied officer's quarters he came to. As he was one level away from the bridge, he was right next to their living quarters.

The first room he came to looked empty on first glance, he was halfway across the room before he noticed the sleeping figure in the bed. Jarrek pulled his sword and knife in smooth, fast motions and slowly approached the bed.

He was standing next to the bed, ready to plunge his blade home when he noticed that there was no breath coming from the body. What the hell? Going to the computer, he checked the duty roster and found all but Varill's personal security confined to their rooms by Commander Varill himself.

What was Varill playing at? Confident that he had found the reason for the empty corridors, although clueless for the reasoning, Jarrek continued towards the bridge and Varill himself. Varill without realizing it was aiding in his own destruction.

Not two minutes later, Jarrek realized he should have kept the stealth, as he was bounding down the hallways towards his objective, he was running right into Varill's personal guard. They made sure that Jarrek regretted losing his caution before they presented him to Varill's brand of greeting. They surrounded him and the leader grabbed one arm while another did the same to his other side. Wondering what was going on and about to morph out of the group, they stabbed him in the chest with a needle and pushed the plunger. His body immediately burned and his symbiot screamed inside his head. Shit! They did have a way to disable their morph. They proceeded to beat him around the face and ribs, before dragging him to Varill and dropping him at his feet. He quickly engaged his comm unit, so that his team knew he was taken and to save his brother and daughter.

14.

That Simple?

Hailey ran into Sidhawk just as she was leaving the Goddess' chapel. She was so happy to see him she immediately smiled and jumped into his arms and planted a big kiss on his cheek. "I am so happy to see you! I need your help. Jarrek is about to make a bone-headed move and I need to save his ass, so we can live happily-ever-after."

Sidhawk saw Hailey exit the Goddesses chambers and was surprised she had found it. They had tucked it away in this section on purpose. This way, ensured that the ugliness of their war did not reach her. She was unsullied by their fight and no warrior would come here unless cleansed from any battle. When Hailey had looked up at him and smiled, he was surprised again. Then she astounded him by jumping into his arms and kissing his cheek. What was going on? She had just left from a tense scene where Loku was being an idiot with tears on her face. He expected that he would need to comfort her and even cheer her up before they could discuss what had happened. "You are well Hailey?" He asked tentatively.

"Fine and dandy, Sid, let's get started. How do I work the bond?" Hailey questioned. Sidhawk looked confused, and she needed him to keep up.

"Look, Sid, I don't have time to play twenty questions with you. I need you to tell me how to work my bond with Jarrek. Keep up here. Things are happening at a rapid pace and I need to be in time. I have a wedding to plan and I need to make sure the groom will live to be there."

"Wedding, groom, twenty questions game? I do not understand your speech Hailey, what is going on in a fast manner? If you can tell me plainly what is happening, then I will be glad to assist you." Sidhawk had tried to understand her speech, but she was talking rapidly and practically dragging him back down the hall towards her room. He needed a clearer understanding of her language. He vowed to spend hours with her learning all the ins and out of her language, if he only could live through whatever she was planning now.

"I want you to tell me how to work the bond that Jarrek and I have so that I can let him know that I love him and accept the bond, before he lets Varill kill him to give me a freedom I don't want. Savvy?" Hailey told Sidhawk, adding a little Captain Jack there at the end, just to tweak his nose. She loved how so many of those she had spoken with had such difficulties understanding her language. It had her laughing on the inside so much that she was surprised she hadn't peed herself yet.

"Oh, yes. Of course, I will try. We may need to find Loku and ask whom the eldest man aboard is. I have knowledge, but no practical experience you know. No one has had a Cordisa in thousands of ansis', we may need help." Sidhawk was so happy to hear that she changed her mind, he was reluctant to ask what had changed her mind, but as she was dragging him along at a fast pace he was not sure if he should. She may need to slow to catch her breath for the explanation, if that was the case, then he should ask.

"May I ask what has happened to change your mind? Not that I am complaining mind you, I am just curious." Sidhawk decided that he had nothing to lose in asking, so went ahead and did just that.

"I met your Goddess while I was visiting her and she told me to get over myself, because she really had made Jarrek just for me or me for Jarrek I guess since he's older." Hailey told him matter of fact.

Sidhawk stopped dead at her words. The Goddess had spoken with Hailey? Wow. "She really spoke to you?" He asked in a voice full of awe.

"Yes, really Sid, like I would make something like that up. Jeez! Look, the point is that she told me that Jarrek and I were supposed to be together and that if I wanted to keep that love I would need to learn about the bond, as he had made a bone-headed decision and was about to die if I didn't figure it out." Hailey told him pulling at his arm in an unsuccessful attempt to move him along.

"Wow. Hailey you are going to tell me all about it. This is momentous!" Sidhawk replied, excited.

"Move your ass, Sid and I will tell you when we save Jarrek." Hailey told him and finally succeeded in getting him to continue moving.

Sidhawk directed her left when she was going to turn to the right, certain that her room and the lift to the bridge was that direction. "My rooms and by extension the elevator to the bridge is to the right Sid. Where are you taking me?" Hailey inquired.

"There is more than one lift Hailey, I am simply getting us there faster." Sidhawk replied in the sarcastic tone of voice he had heard Hailey use on more than one occasion.

"Snark, Sid? Progress, I like it. Of course, there is more than one elevator to the bridge. I should have realized. Sorry." Hailey said and rolled her eyes at her mistake.

Not even thirty seconds later, they were striding onto the bridge and Hailey was calling for Loku. Loku took one look at her face, stopped what he originally was going to say, and instead asked, "How may I help you, Hailey?"

"I need to know who can tell me how to use the bond that Jarrek and I share. I need him to stop his bone-headed move and get his ass back onboard this ship." Hailey told Loku, for now skipping over their earlier scene in an effort to concentrate on what was more important. Saving Jarrek's very sexy behind.

"I can tell you what my father told me. We have mayhap a handful of men that could describe the use of the bond. If you will give me three minutes, I will have them come to the war room. While we wait, perhaps you will do me the courtesy of telling me what has happened?" Loku was happy that she was not tearing into him over their earlier meeting, but he was still the First Officer and in charge of this ship in Jarrek's absence. He led Hailey and Sidhawk towards the war room while he gestured for his aid to send out the necessary messages to the older crewmembers.

Sidhawk stepped up and answered the questions Loku had. "Hailey has spoken to the Goddess, who has assured her that she and Jarrek are meant to be together, however, Jarrek is in danger and if Hailey cannot figure out how to work the bond, so that Jarrek is aware that she is willing to accept him and their bond, Jarrek will succeed in getting Varill to kill him."

"The Goddess spoke to Hailey? That is amazing!" Loku exclaimed and then the rest of what Sidhawk said kicked in. "I knew that no good cruvek was going to do something stupid." He growled.

"Yes, Loku, we can all growl at him later. Tell me quickly what your daddy told you." Hailey said and rolled her eyes at him, before taking Jarrek's seat at the table.

"Well my father did not tell me much. He only said that if I were ever lucky enough to find a Cordisa, I was to close my eyes and think of her, all that we are to each other. We are essentially the same person through the bond and it should not be a struggle to understand the other half of ourselves." Loku told her.

"Save me from existential garbage please. I need clear and precise instructions. I don't speak woo-woo." Hailey snarked to Loku, and wondered why did the damn instructions to stuff that was really, really important have to come wrapped in nonsense or mystic haiku crap?

"I do not know the language woo-woo, so was not speaking it. What did you mean by that, Hailey?" Loku asked, as confused as others by her weird speech.

"I meant that I don't understand the instructions Loku. Can you please explain it to me again, in a way that I can understand it?" Hailey explained, not even bothering to explain what she really meant. Now was not the time for the language issue to crop up. She had to save Jarrek. She was starting to get a horrible feeling in her gut.

Loku was about to try again, when the chime sounded for entry. Giving permission, he welcomed the warriors and asked them to take a seat. "Briefly, as we are short on time I will say that the woman seated with us is Jarrek's Cordisa and they have just bonded a couple of hours ago. The Goddess has spoken with Hailey and let her know that Jarrek is in trouble and about to get himself killed. She is looking for information on how to work their bond so that Jarrek knows to come back to the ship immediately as Hailey does love him and will accept the bond. We need any information that you can give to us on how that this can be accomplished quickly. Did I miss anything Hailey, or is there anything you wish to add about the situation at hand?" Loku asked turning to her.

"No Loku, I believe that sums it up. I will need you to be very specific with me on how to reach the bond. Cryptic information is a waste of my time and not something I am willing to try to deal with." Hailey told the waiting men.

They all looked to each other for a moment and then turned back to her and said the same thing at the same time. "Just close your eyes and think of your bonded mate."

"Seriously? Just close my eyes and think of Jarrek?" Hailey tried to verify with them. It sounded too simple. She didn't want mystic woo-woo crap, but thought it would be a little harder than that.

"I am not sure you understand exactly what a bond entails, Your Highness. You and Jarrek are now one. The same person, but separate. You should be able to feel what he feels, experience what he does, and know what is around him and how to change it. It is the same with him. He should know how you feel, what is going on around you and what he needs to do to change it or fix it, if it requires fixing. However, if he is being hurt or tortured, he may try to keep you out. Not that he will be successful, but he can limit you somewhat on the access side. You just have to be more determined." Calmron B'el Sassony tried to explain the bond to her in a way that he hoped she would understand.

"Oh determination won't be a problem. I was told by the Goddess that I need to let him know that I accept him or he will get himself killed." Hailey said in a dry tone of voice. That caused all of the warriors to murmur their astonishment that she had met the Goddess. Hailey didn't understand what the big deal was.

"Well everyone needs to pipe down. I am going to try to let him know right now." Hailey said as she called for quiet. She mentally crossed her fingers and tried to reach Jarrek. Thinking of the way his skin felt against hers. How warm it was and the delicious sent of his skin when he surrounded her with his body. The drugging influence of his kiss and the way she felt as he filled her with his cock. Feeling the tingle begin to cover her skin, she knew somehow that it was working. She was reaching him on a level she never knew could exist between a couple. She tried to sink into his body and be Jarrek, so that she could perhaps slip inside his mind and he could absorb the love she felt for him. The conversation she had had with the Goddess, and that she really wanted him to come back to her. Except, she found pain, broken ribs and a scream of "NO!", ringing in her head, before everything leading up to that moment, just seemed to rewind and show her in fast forward what had occurred.

15.

A Little Torture

"Ahh, Jarrek. My very old friend. How wonderful it is to see you again. I must say that you are looking much better than the last time I saw you. You are so much prettier when the black and purple starts showing on your skin. I really have to work on your ugly face though. It just begs me for correction. Every time we talk I mean to get started on that, but you look so good in purple, I start with that. My guards have done us both a favor, would not you agree?" Varill questioned after walking around Jarrek and checking the lovely work his guards did. He gestured for a couple of guards to pick him so that he could look Jarrek in his swollen, purple and black eyes.

"Where is my pet? Have you brought back my property?"

Jarrek spit blood at Varill. He hoped that his men could hear that he was a captive and had already left with his daughter, brother and the poor other woman they found. "You will never have my Cordisa Varill. I will see you dead first."

Varill just licked at the blood and enjoyed it. Chuckling a little, he said, "Oh Jarrek, such a manly cliché, how droll. You must have something better than that. Perhaps I should have my men bring your lovely brother in here with us. He has not been as abused as the others with him have, but I have helped him look better. Shall I give you matching looks? No, that would not work on your face. I really must go with the original work I think will make you the most beautiful. But perhaps your brother will help you find your tongue to answer my questions without all of the posturing, hmm?" Varill asked.

"You would have a hard time producing him Varill, as you have been quite lax in your security. There has been no one to challenge me when I came to remove my brother and daughter from your tender care. I have come and gone three times since we last spoke." Jarrek taunted Varill.

Varill screamed for his guards to verify the veracity of Jarrek's claims, but already could tell that he spoke the truth.

"Dammit, Jarrek. I will rain fire on your ship and kill all aboard. Those who do not perish in the first wave will wish they had when I let my guard have them. I may have been lax in my security and should have anticipated that you would try to rescue your brother, but we have recently found such entertaining vids from my pet's home planet, I was a little distracted. The kind that shows how we can penetrate our enemy's with our shafts while simultaneously causing the maximum amount of pain and anguish to bring our hormones to peak. We may even be able to produce females of our kind again. I will be lauded, heralded with the resurrection of our race. First, though I have to get enough of my own young ready. Once I have my own army, dedicated to me only, and not the crown of Yurzzat. I will return and crown myself King. We will conquer my little pet's planet and keep the females for breeding and the men to satisfy our need for pain and humiliation to keep our hormones at peak."

Varill began pulling out his knives and laser cutters, in preparation of making Jarrek more beautiful, before he sent him to meet his creators. Walking over to Jarrek, he carefully made his first cut to his face. Precision was key to creating perfection.

"Lurzar here has been telling me the most amazing tale. That the females of their kind can also be used to torture and penetrate, but that they carry their young inside them and not in eggs. He is working on a female to see if that is true and if he can impregnate her. We will see if she can carry our young. If it is successful, I may just take up residence on my Pet's planet and make it my world entirely. I could create a planet of children dedicated to my rule and me. With my trusted guard and Second here to help me create more females of our kind, we could repopulate the race that you and yours have decimated. Why, do you know that we are a race of practically nothing? We have five such ships like my own here and only the rulers of my planet left and they are cryogenically frozen to preserve the leadership of our people." Varill relayed to Jarrek as he kept his cuts slow and steady.

He wanted to make sure that he got deep enough to really make the changes stick. Varill would have to make sure Jarrek healed with the perfection that he was creating before sending him to his death. He wanted to make sure that Jarrek looked his best for the ridiculous female they worshiped.

"You know my friend; I can already see some improvement to your face. I really feel that you are going to look just perfect when I am through. Let us take a small break and perhaps discuss where my pet is and what you have done while you were on my ship these three different times as you have stated." Varill asked as his guard came back with the knowledge that Kirrek and the daughter were indeed gone. It seems Jarrek had also managed to take Lurzar's playmate, who was being informed of that fact now. "I have been informed of your brother's rescue along with my second's female. Perhaps you can save yourself some pain by telling us where they are?" Varill stepped back as Lurzar came up to Jarrek.

"Where my toy? Want my experiment back now!" Lurzar managed to grit through the slit of his mouth.

"I would never return a female to your care. I would not even give you a luzarian worm. They are far away from you and that is all that matters. I have ships headed this way to join me in blowing you to hell." Jarrek managed to get out from behind a clenched jaw. His teeth were in danger of shattering, so tight a hold did he have on them. They would have to work harder if they wanted him to scream out his pain.

"Perhaps I can help convince you to return what belongs to me. I have watched many of the vids that they have on the little white marble, and they have practices in pain there that are very much to my liking. I think I will share some of them with you."

Lurzar promised him. Looking for permission from Varill, who nodded and sat back in his seat to watch the coming show, his shaft already rising in anticipation.

"Yes, my new King likes that idea very much." Lurzar said and turned Jarrek's head to show him Varill's rising shaft. Stepping back he removed his clothing and walked casually over to the instruments lined up for Varill's use in making Jarrek's new face. "Let us start by removing some of your pretty red skin, and then I will break a few bones and sink my shaft inside you. You may not enjoy this, but we will I assure you. Perhaps his Majesty will avail himself of your body as well. Would not that be nice?"

No! That was the only word screaming inside his head. Perhaps he was hasty in wanting Varill to kill him. His body began to tingle and he felt relieved all of the sudden. Closing his eyes, he allowed himself to sink inside his body to figure out what was going on and found himself with his Cordisa in the Goddesses' chapel. He felt her confusion and love for him and was so happy to know that she did love him. Jarrek watched as the Goddess came alive and spoke with her, Holy Goddess above! They were beyond blessed that she had come to them. Hailey was going to accept their bond; she just had to save him from being an idiot. Jarrek watched as Hailey spoke to Loku and some of his other warriors about how to work the bond and her relief that she was able to reach him.

"Too late, my love. I am sorry that I failed you, failed to give you time and a choice. I wish that I could escape and come back to you, but they have found a way to kill my symbiot's ability to morph away from here. I am too late; I love you and will see you on the other side when it is your time to come join me. Please let our daughter know of the love that we have for one another and her." Jarrek pushed his thoughts and feelings to her along their bond. He ignored all that was being done to the outside of his body; it no longer mattered what they did, he was about to join the Goddess and if she allowed it, watch and protect Hailey and their daughter.

16.

To Save a Corduva

Marthos had just completed his secondary mission and was heading back to the ship when he ran into Bruthus and Rometho. Each signaled the completion of their missions and were turning back to the ship when Jarrek's comm engaged and they listened to his capture and beating. They all raced back to the ship to see if the others heard the capture as well and to come up with a plan.

There they found a controlled type of chaos as Sameth worked to save the small little female. She looked as though she came from the same marble that Hailey had, but her body painted a clear picture that she was not left unaware of the things happening to her, nor was she spared their torture. She was missing skin from her breasts, stomach and thighs from what they could see. She was not as lush and round as Hailey and her skin was not as dark. In fact she looked almost translucent her skin was so fair. Her black hair did not help darken her skin. The small female had her hair shorn to her head in a spiky style and they wondered if the Krakill had cut her hair off as part of their torture. They felt horrible and said a prayer to the Goddess to watch over the little one.

"Did you hear the Commander's capture?" Marthos asked into the frenzy.

"Yes. Shemrick and I were just discussing what we should do, if anything." Heathrick replied still watching over the small little female he had saved.

"I was charged with returning Kirrek and the Commander's daughter back to the ship with all haste if something should happen to him. I just wondered if we should leave a volunteer behind to rescue him if there is an opportunity." Marthos said looking around at each face.

Hearing a sound back at the entrance hatch, they all froze and pulled their weapons. Bruthus and Rometho going back the way they came. Seeing Darthos they let out a breath and released the tension that had turned their bodies into killing machines. They saw the state he was in, turned, and led the way back into the medical bay, re-sheathing weapons as they walked. They knew that he would have to wait for medical attention, but they could get him strapped to a berth and ready him for Sameth's attention.

They should have brought another medical officer with them. Sameth was only one person and with the little human, Kirrek and now Darthos injured and needing attention, he would need a few extra hands. Fortunately, although they were both severely injured, they were not in danger of dying and Sameth could spend all of his energies on saving the female.

When the other warrior's did not hear fighting but instead them returning back to medical they wondered what is was they had heard before Darthos came into view, slowly dragging his battered body into medical. Marthos turned to Bruthus and said, "I believe that you should get us out of here, Captain. We must return to the ship in all haste. I want our Princess safe and the small female may need more attention than Sameth will be able to provide on the small amount of medical supplies that we have. I am charged with their safety and have agreed to follow his directive." Marthos hoped he was up to the challenge that Jarrek had given to him. Kirrek would probably be the hardest to convince.

Bruthus looked at Marthos, not really surprised by his Commander's directive. When you were lucky enough to find your Cordisa you made plans for every contingency. Taking one last look at the small female who continued to capture his attention, he went to get them back to the Sh'dow al D'th. "Poor little thing, Goddess protect and watch over her." Bruthus prayed as he took his seat and began his stealth maneuvers to get them back home.

The return trip seemed to go by so much faster, even though Marthos was actually tenser than when they started out. Sending a small bubble of encrypted messages when they were ten verls from the ship, he hoped they would have enough time to complete the directives. He had alerted Loku that their mission was successful and that medical needed to be alerted to the little humans' needs along with Kirrek, Darthos and the Princess. He had included the news of Jarrek's capture and the directive given to him from Jarrek as regards Kirrek, Hailey and the Princess. He was sure that he would need help in keeping that promise.

"There is an incoming message for you, sir." A voice said through the speaker of the comm, situated at the head of the table in front of Hailey. Looking down at the speaker, than up to Loku, she said, "Jarrek has been captured by Varill and is hurt pretty bad. Now his second in command, Lurzar or Lazur or whatever he's called is hurting Jarrek for information on a female that our guys may have rescued, but they have hurt very badly." Hailey blinked rapidly, coming out of the dual experience. It was going to take some getting used to, without making her want to hurl. It had made her a little dizzy.

Loku leaned over the table and pushed the response button. "Please send it to me here." He commanded. Two seconds later a beep came through and Loku pressed a button and put the message on the big screen to the left of the table on the wall. They all read the contents quickly, and cheered for the successful retrieval of Kirrek, Darthos, and her daughter, who it shocked her, to realize was these men's Princess. The condition of the woman shocked them all. Hailey was suddenly grateful that she was not awake or aware of what happened to her and felt horribly guilty that she had not suffered like this other woman. Which was silly, she thought to herself, but she felt it just the same.

Loku looked over at the older men seated at the table and thanked them for their service and then dismissed them. He then summoned his aid into the room and began issuing orders for medical to meet the incoming ship with three gurneys to transport the wounded and their best medical personnel to meet the ship to transfer the Princess to the suite set aside for her care. Second Senior Medical Doctor Krases B'el Whalekin would be overseeing every moment of her care as soon as she touched down. Not only was he an excellent medical healer, but Sameth had chosen him to study every single document that they had in the data chips for infants, women and embryonic development. He now possessed all the knowledge that they would need to keep the Princess alive until she could be born, and he would make sure, down to the cellular level that she was perfectly healthy. They were all terrified that the Krakill had managed to harm her somehow. It was something those evil bastards were certainly capable of. Every warrior was holding his breath and saying prayers to the Goddess to let her be healthy and strong.

"Would you like to go meet the ship?" Loku asked Hailey.

"No, I would like to speak to Sid for a moment and then you." Hailey told him.

"Then if you will excuse me, I will call for refreshments and return." Loku said and gave her a small bow with his hand over his heart.

"Sid, I know that you want to get to the ship or medical to meet and check on your man, but I want to ask about the message from Marthos. He has specifically said that these instructions come from Jarrek and outline that Kirrek is to take my daughter and me to your planet and she is to be taught what is needed to rule. Is this something that is necessary? Why will I not be able to take her home with me?" Hailey questioned Sidhawk as he had stepped into her confidant role and had been honest in all he said. He had taken the time to get to know her and let her get to know him. Jarrek hadn't even done that. To be fair, they had been caught up in this mess, but still.

"Jarrek is your Corduva, and must make plans for every contingency, including his death. He is ensuring you are taken care of and that you have all you could possibly require. Of course you will have to come to our planet Hailey, do you keep forgetting that your daughter is a Princess and Jarrek's heir? He is the next ruler of our planet. When he passes to the next plane, his daughter will rule after him. If he passes to the next plane before she has come of age, then Jarrek appoints a guardian to teach her how to rule the throne and takes care of that throne until she is of age to take over those duties. I am quite sure that you are part of that ruling body as you are his Princess now that you are bonded. Kirrek is his brother and can be trusted to rule for your daughter without trying to usurp her place, or yours." Sidhawk explained as patiently as he could while inside he was ready to race off and kick Kirrek's ass. He heartily approved of Jarrek's provisions. It would force Kirrek to stop his rush towards death and keep him safe. Not that he wanted Jarrek to die. Goddess no, but perhaps he could order his brother to refrain from missions and help train his daughter. Sidhawk was tired of space. There was nothing to see, even when they found a trading post or moon to search and they could stretch their legs. Very few planets were capable of sustaining life, so there were not as many where they could spend a few weeks in the crisp air.

"Thanks Sid. You can go to Kirrek. Kick his ass sweetie. Doesn't matter if he is hurting, kick him more. That way he can do all his healing at one time. I doubt you would go so far as to kill him, but he needs to see you fierce honey, or he will walk all over you." Hailey told him, standing up to give him a gentle hug. She only reached his collarbone.

"You are a wonderful woman Hailey. Jarrek was really lucky that the Goddess gave him you." Sidhawk said and kissed the top of her head.

Hailey blushed, but was pleased with the compliment. "I think we both got lucky. I hope you do as well, Sid. Don't worry too much. I remember all that you told me about bonded couples and it will be all right." She watched him walk out the doors to chase after his man. She hoped he did kick Kirrek.

"He is correct, you know. Jarrek did get lucky that the Goddess gave you to him." Loku said from the opposite doorway, surprising Hailey.

"What? I thought I was Satan incarnate, or the great big evil, inconsiderate and uncouth." Hailey replied, trying not to show her surprise at his watching her talk to Sidhawk.

"I was angry and panicked that my best friend of the last fourteen hundred years was inconsolable when you broke his heart. Jarrek was talking about killing himself or letting Varill kill him so that you could be free. I did not stop to consider your side. I did not care about your side. I only wanted to help my friend, and yes, my past lover. I am apologizing to you, that I did not stop to think of all that you had gone through. You have my most heartfelt apologies, my Queen." Loku said in his most solemn tone and bowed deeply with his hand over his heart. He held that pose for a moment before straightening his spine.

"Look, Loku. I get it, really. I would have probably done the same thing if I were in your shoes. If my best friend came to me and cried on my shoulder, then I would rip the person to pieces. I wouldn't care if it was her fault or his fault, or all a big misunderstanding. If she was crying and hurt then I would hurt him just because he made her cry. You basically did what I would do. It hurt. I cried and then I thought about it after I talked with the Goddess. We're cool. No need to apologize, but I accept it and give my apologies to you. I am sorry Loku." Hailey told him and then stepped closer to give him a big hug. Once she stepped back she looked up at him and said, "Let's sit back down. You alien bastards are too tall for me to keep looking up, it hurts my neck. At least at the table it is a little better. I don't feel as though I have to strain my neck to look at you." Hailey sat down and continued.

"So Sidhawk explained to me exactly what a bonded couple can do for each other and I have a plan. I am quite sure you won't like it, but I am telling you right now, this is how it will be. Your job will be to back me up. I am coming to you with this for two reasons. One, you are Jarrek's best friend as we have already established. Second, because as you pointed out earlier, you are the Second in Command of this ship." Hailey told him once he had seated himself across from her.

"What have you come up with? I will tell you right now that if is risky I will stop you. Jarrek would kill me if I did not." Loku shot right back.

Hailey rolled her eyes at him. Men were the same everywhere it seemed. They really liked to puff out their chests and make big sweeping decrees. They were clueless. "I plan on using the bond to morph to Jarrek when he is close to death and morph him to safety." Hailey new this would work. The only problem was that she was having a hard time not trying it now. She was here with Loku having this conversation, but also with Jarrek suffering unthinkable torture. She was trying to reassure him that it didn't usually last long and then they would give him a break, but didn't think that he cared. He kept trying to push her out so that she didn't have to suffer with him. She pushed some of her own terrors at him, so that she could reassure him she knew of what she spoke. He only got angry and wanted to morph away so that he could seek revenge on her behalf. Then became even angrier when he realized the drug they had given him was still killing his ability to morph at all. "The problem I have and wanted to speak to you about are that the Krakill have found a way to prevent your kind from morphing. They have given Jarrek some kind of drug that burns his symbiot and has rendered him without his extra abilities. I need to know what kind of effect this will have on us when I try to save him." Hailey asked coming back to herself again. She briefly wondered what she looked like when she was pushing stuff along the bond, then pushed it away. Too many things going on to let herself get sidetracked.

"Unknown. I do not think that it should be an issue, as if he is close to death, than as his bonded you can morph to him and morph him out. Unless they are right there to give you an injection within the three seconds that you are there, I do not see it as an issue." Loku said after a moment to contemplate all the issues. That they had found a way to stop their morphing was the most horrifying fact. He wanted to start firing on the ship to wipe that information out of existence. Only Jarrek's presence onboard stopped him from giving that order.

"Great. I was thinking along those lines as well. Now, how do we go about this? Sidhawk didn't tell me how far I could morph to, when I went to his side and then morphed away. Can I morph from our ship to theirs without a problem? Can I morph back that far with Jarrek?" Hailey questioned and hoped for the best.

"No Hailey, that is too far. If you were on a planet, it would be possible to go from one side to the other without a problem as bonded couples are very strong together, but with his symbiot unable to morph at all, you would be doing it all under your own strength. There is just no way that a novice could do something like that. You do not even know how to morph." Loku told her shaking his head almost before she finished the question.

"Well I was hoping for good news. So, how can I save Jarrek and get us back onboard before we blow the ship. We are running out of time. I feel it slipping with every minute that Jarrek is still in Varill's hands." Hailey was beginning to get scared that she had waited too long to get her head straight, but then took a deep breath and forced it away. Part of that was Jarrek freaking out at the idea of her anywhere near Varill. "Too freaking bad," She pushed back towards Jarrek. He wasn't in a position to deny her.

"Hurry Loku, I'm not kidding about time running out soon." Hailey said again, feeling the dread balloon bigger in her stomach.

"Let's get to the launch bay. We can get Bruthus to bring you back closer to Varill's ship. I will send Marthos and Rometho with you to help you nurse Jarrek's injuries while getting you back to the ship with all haste. Rometho can also calculate how far away you have to be before you blow the ship."

Loku practically dragged her down the hall. She felt as though she was a stuffed toy he was pulling, just flopping along boneless. They reached the elevator and Loku called for landing bay twelve. Thirty seconds later the elevator open to many people shouting and moving around very quickly.

"What's going on?" She was scared the Krakill was attacking them.

"This is just the typical chaos of a returning ship with injured men. That we have an injured woman, and the Princess on board that ship, well it is making all the men rush to get the ship docked correctly and the medical personnel ready to take their charges as soon as that is accomplished. Look to the left. They just finished backing into the bay. Now, they are ready to take charge of the injured. As soon as they complete that I will get them ready to head back out with you." Loku had to speak up, before he was heard above the shouting of orders.

She watched as the back door lowered to the ground with a dull thunk, before it had completely touched the floor two men were jumping on board towards Sameth and his first patient. It was the other woman from earth.

Horrified by the condition of her body, she screamed up at Loku that the woman should be covered from the warriors' eyes. She would not appreciate a bunch of men seeing her so vulnerable. She hated that a large group of them had seen her naked and vulnerable. That they had not looked at her differently did not matter. She thought that they had also kept their promise not to talk about it, but still that didn't matter to the main issue of not wanting to be seen so vulnerable. No woman would want that. Sure, a lot of them were medical personnel and had to see the injuries to treat them, but the rest of these warriors did not need to see that poor woman like that.

Loku gave a loud whistle and told them to cover her up and just like that she was covered and they were rolling her away to the medical ward at top speed. Next were

Kirrek and the other warrior with him. She wished she could remember the name that Marthos said in the message, but figured that if she was successful in rescuing Jarrek, she could meet him later, and if she failed then she would be in Hell and want to die, so it would be the last thought on her mind.

Sidhawk ran alongside Kirrek's stretcher, cataloguing his injuries with his eyes, but keeping a tight grip on his hand. She knew that grip. It was the grip of a lover trying to keep the beloved tied to the plane of living. A grip that said he was not going to give up and let Kirrek succumb to his injuries. Hailey prayed she would be able to grip Jarrek like that. She was still going to kick his ass for being stupid.

The last group of medical personnel seemed to be the largest. Hailey began to move closer. She knew what this was going to be, her daughter. She was terrified and grateful that so many were there for her unborn child. Loku, sensing that she was overwhelmed with emotions, wrapped an arm around her to give her comfort. She took the warmth gratefully. She hoped that

Jarrek was with her, watching as she got the first look of their daughter. The baby was growing rapidly, which scared her more than a little. She was technically only about three days conceived, but she looked as though she was closer to twenty-two weeks, or four and a half months along. When she had first seen the video from Mr. Stinky the baby had looked about eight, 9 weeks, or two months along. That had worried her, as she couldn't fathom how so much time could have passed and her not be aware of it, but that she was a mom at all had filled her with love, panic and fear. Now she could hold this baby in the palm of her hand. She looked like a little miniature person. Just forming eyelashes and brows covered her face, and she was currently sucking her thumb and kicking her legs. You could see the vulva quite clearly. Holy moly this was real. She wished her mom could see this. "Loku, can you ask them to record everything? I want to be able to show my mom how she grew and developed. She would love to see this." Hailey whispered to him while tracing the outside of the glass. She knew that time was running out for Jarrek, but looking at the daughter that while engineered from their genetic material, was awe-inspiring. She wished every mother could watch their child grow inside them like this. It was mesmerizing. She just wanted to sit and stare at the miracle of her child and watch her grow.

"Of course they will Hailey. Jarrek will wish to watch it as well do you not think? Let them take care of your daughter now, Hailey. I promise they will let no harm come to her. Once you rescue her Prati, he will want to see her. Come on, let them in." Loku said while trying to steer her away.

She let her fingers fall from the glass and turned to the man in charge of her care. "Guard her well and record everything please." She told him with tears in her eyes. She was not a mother in the typical sense where the baby was growing inside her, but she felt her daughter all the way to her soul.

Wiping the tears from her face, not ashamed in the least of her emotions for her child, she looked over to the remaining men on the ship. Bruthus, Marthos, Rometho and the twins Heathrick and Shemrick were all there looking back at her. She quickly stepped forward and told them the plan of what she and Loku thought to do. Bruthus turned and began charging the fuel so that they could be on their way as soon as possible.

Heathrick and Shemrick volunteered to go to medical for healiogel and other materials they would need to replenish what had been used on the flight back here, and disappeared out the doors soon after.

Rometho was quiet and turned to calculate the distance needed before they safely blew the Krakill ship without harming Hailey. He would have risked any warrior there and blown it up as soon as possible, including his commander and Prince, Jarrek but he would never risk her. Hailey had charmed him with her small stature and large personality. She had such fire to her, that he was jealous of his Commander.

Marthos was the toughest sell. He had agreed to take charge of Hailey, to see that she remained safe and delivered immediately to his uncle and King. He had to agree though with Loku's passionate explanation, that now that Hailey and Jarrek had bonded, if he was near death, she would automatically try to morph to save him. If they were not close to help, then she was doomed along with Jarrek. It was the only argument that they could have used to persuade him to allow the mission to continue.

Unfortunately, he made the mistake of saying that aloud. Once his face stopped stinging he automatically covered his privates as she threatened him with castration. He well remembered her definition of that word to the crew of the bridge. He would have to avoid her for a while. He would take no chances with his manhood. He liked everything right where it was.

God save her from men. Well, make that Goddess save her from men. Postulating peacocks every one of them. She hoped he felt her slap for a month. She felt she extra prizes for hitting anyone of the behemoths as they all topped her by a foot and a half deserved an extra award. She may have been round, but she could jump and had excellent aim.

"Move out. I have a mate to rescue."

Bruthus nodded and checked to see how much fuel had recharged. Pleased to see that they were close to full. They would easily be back before there was a danger of them running out of fuel. "We are good on my end." He told Hailey, getting back in the ship and readying it for immediate departure.

"Excellent. All we need are supplies from medical and we can go. Rometho you can work on your calculations on the ship, right?" she asked, turning towards him.

"I am almost finished with them now, but can definitely finish during the flight." Rometho told Hailey with a smile. He was going to have to go to her small marble and look for one of his own.

Heathrick and Shemrick came back in with a cart piled with medical supplies. She started grabbing supplies as soon as they got to the ship. They were loaded and ready to depart within another two minutes. Loku wished them all luck and stepped out of the ship to return to the bridge. Heathrick asked Hailey if she thought she would need them, as they thought to watch over the little female they had rescued.

"No Heathrick, you guys go ahead, although I appreciate the offer. Is the other woman your Cordisa?" She asked as she strapped in with Marthos' help.

"No, she is not our Cordisa, but we still feel responsible for her well-being. She is small and looked very bad. We both want to go with you and get revenge for her harsh treatment. Lurzar needs a beating for sure, but we will stay and watch over her. The bombs are set and she will have her revenge, although more merciful than what he deserves." Heathrick told her while Shemrick just nodded when he finished speaking.

"Thanks for watching over her guys, if she wakes before I come back let her know I will visit her as soon as possible."

She requested of them as they had turned to walk off the ship. She only got a raised hand for an acknowledgement. Three minutes later they were away she was amazed at how little jostling there was. Although, this left her with too much silence and time to concentrate on what was happening to her man.

Rometho went to the front and spoke with Bruthus is low tones, probably telling him the distance they needed before they could blow the ship.

Meanwhile Hailey was focusing on what was happening with Jarrek. He was lying on a weird table that looked more like an architect's drawing table completely nude, with his wrists tied above his head. Varill watched from the side, as naked as Jarrek and lazily stroking himself, as he watched her beloved being tortured. Lurzar had broken the tibia and femur of his right leg. He was now working on cutting long jagged lines into Jarrek's chest, down his abdomen and almost to his pubic area. The closer he came to that tender area the more Jarrek cried out. He knew that was what they wanted and tried to deny them, but Goddess it hurt.

Hailey felt as though she should be panting with the pain, but while she felt it, Jarrek was doing his best to block her from the agony. She was having a hard time deciding if she was grateful she wasn't feeling all of the pain, or angry that he wouldn't let her share the burden. She distracted herself with the compelling arguments on both sides while she waited for them to get close enough she could morph to Jarrek and then back. Let it be soon, she prayed. Her body was pushing her to morph to him.

Bruthus called out from the front that they were within six minutes of their target. Hailey looked to Marthos and Rometho and asked, "Does that mean I can morph to Jarrek safely?"

"Yes." They both answered. Bruthus spoke up from the front though before she could try. "Wait, Hailey. I want to turn the ship back around, so that we are automatically headed away from the ship.

This should give us a few more seconds to get clear before we blow up the ship. Every parasec is going to count on this one." He told her.

"Let me know when. Someone give me a knife to cut the rope binding him to the table he is on, I am monitoring him now and Lurzar just stepped away from Jarrek. I can't tell if he is picking up another instrument of if something worse is coming, but we are about to lose the best moment to do this." Hailey replied with her eyes closed. She was trying to force her body to hold off just another few seconds, but her symbiot knew they were about to lose their best opportunity. Someone slipped a blade into her hand so that she gripped the pommel of the blade.

"Now." Bruthus said and she didn't hesitate, but immediately let her body do exactly what it had been trying to force her to do for the last hour and morphed straight to Jarrek's side. He looked horrible and Hailey hated to touch him, but she quickly cut the bonds holding him to the table and wrapped her arms around him as tight as she could and looked into Varill's astonished face. "So long fucker!" she cried before morphing them both to safety. Hailey never saw Lurzar, or how close he came to capturing both of them. She landed with a painful jolt back on the ship, with Jarrek on top of her, pushing her painfully into the seat that she had been sitting on. He immediately started to fall backwards towards the floor, and she knew that he was going to drag her on top of him. She didn't want him to be hurt further, so shouted for Marthos and Rometho to help her.

They each grabbed an arm and dragged him to the back of the ship. She called out to Bruthus that they were on board, so that he could get them home as fast as possible. She was making her way back to medical to help the Rometho and Marthos care for Jarrek, when the ship rocked violently. She threw her arms straight out to catch herself from smacking head first into a wall. "What the hell?" she hollered and changed direction to go up front with Bruthus.

"Everyone brace for impact. Varill thought that he was sending a hit towards the Sh'dow al D'th, but found us instead. I am now completely visible to their ship and going as fast as possible away from them. I expect another blast at any moment. I will try to evade if possible, but strap in for a bumpy ride." Bruthus sent out over the intercom. Hailey reached the cockpit and sat down next to him, strapping in.

"How can I help?" She asked.

Bruthus looked over at Hailey and then did a double take. "Are you hurt?" he asked quickly.

She glanced down at herself and saw all the blood that had freaked out Bruthus. "No, I'm okay. This is Jarrek's blood. They did a real number on him. I want to be in there checking on him and helping them, but I figured I should stay out of the way. You guys are probably well versed in triage on one another." She told him, then repeated her original question of, "How can I help?"

Bruthus turned his head back and watched his screens, maneuvering around the shots that Varill was throwing at them. "Right now, just say a prayer to the Goddess that I can get us all back to the ship alive."

"Do you have any defensive capabilities on this ship? I understand it is a stealth ship, but surely you designed it with weapons?" She looked at the consoles readouts and joysticks. It reminded her greatly of a fighter pilot game she used to play with her male friends in high school. They went off to be military fighter pilots and this looked just like the games that they played. She just needed to figure out what joystick ran the targeting and which buttons were the weapons and what kind.

"It does have weapons, but I can't run that system and still manually move the ship from the blasts from Varill's ship." Bruthus told her. Smiling a little that Hailey, who was such a small, little female thought to help fight. He would have laughed aloud, but heard her threaten Marthos and all of the bridge crew. He did not want her to target his balls next, so managed to swallow the mirth.

"Duh, Bruthus! Please do not act all stupid with me. I found the targeting stick, which button is what type of weapon? Do you have counter-measures to draw their fire from the ship? If so, is it the high left button above the control stick? What about missiles, or lasers, or even bulleted machine guns?" She asked in rapid bursts.

Seeing that Hailey was serious about trying to help, he swallowed his original laughter and thought to himself, "I have got to find myself one just like her." His mind tried to go to the female that they had rescued, but he pushed it away. He then proceeded to tell her what button did what and watched in awe as she began to meet each burst head on, so that he didn't have to move the ship around in jerky movements to get out of the way. They were beginning to gain distance from Varill's ship and he waited with his breath held until they were in the range that Rometho had calculated. As soon as he crossed that distance, he sent out the frequency to blow Varill straight to Hell. He quickly told Marthos and Rometho that he had just detonated the bombs and to expect shockwaves.

Hailey cheered to hear they had done it. She immediately broke out into song with "We are the Champions of the World" by Queen, causing Bruthus to look at her strange and shake his head. Hailey had to change the words a little so that it was "We are the Champions of the Universe" instead. She belted out the lyrics for Bruthus's amusement while he pushed a whole lot of buttons and took them back to the ship.

Bruthus sent a message to Loku of their success and immediate return with Jarrek seriously wounded. He added that he did not know how urgent his care was, as he had not seen him yet, but that Hailey was soaked in blood.

He added his report on how Hailey had helped with the weapons portion of their flight and the ships desperate need for repairs. Knowing that it would cause many raised brows and plenty of disbelief. If he had not seen for himself her incredible bravery, or how well she had picked up what she needed to do to overcome their situation, he would not believe it either. He would have sent that warrior to the ship's doctors for an evaluation.

They were very close to the Sh'dow al D'th when the first shockwave hit them. It sent them wobbling a little before he smoothed it out and approached the docking bay. They had done it. They were victorious and Varill would trouble them no more. His only regret was that he was unable to see the explosion for himself. That would have been a great treat. He would inquire if anyone had thought to record it happening.

As soon as he had docked, he turned to Hailey who was undoing her own straps and said, "It was an honor to fight with you, my Queen. Are all the women of your planet like you?" He asked and his mind turned to the female they had rescued. He had felt something strange when he saw her, but was not sure what it was.

"No. We are all different. Some are good, bad, selfish, mean and so on. We are a diverse race. We have different religions and colors to our skin, hair and eyes. We are a race of unique individuals. That is why I both love and hate my people."

"Bruthus, if you believe anything else I tell you, believe this; never, ever under estimate just what a woman is capable of. We are warriors, pilots, nurses, mothers, and anything that you can think of. We can do anything we put our mind to and will not let a man dictate to us what we can do. We will make up our own minds and Goddess help you if you get in our way."

With that warning ringing in the air between them, she went to meet up with Marthos and Rometho so that she could be with Jarrek as they took him to medical. He was still alive, and that was all she cared about for now.

17.

An Unexpected Passenger

Jarrek shifted carefully under the blanket, ready to freeze the moment it hurt too much. When nothing hurt too badly he was relieved and worried that he had been out of it for too long. Opening his eyes, he had to blink a few times for everything to come into focus.

He was in his own quarters. Should he not be in medical? He remembered the pain of Lurzar cutting his way down his body. The pain when Lurzar began breaking the bones in his leg. Looking down and pulling the sheet from his naked body, Jarrek was surprised to see only small fading lines of pink. He did not think they would even leave much of a scar. Not that he cared over much for a few new scars. They were battle prizes and something of which to be proud. Not even his ribbed pinched or warned him to take it easy.

Pushing himself up against the headboard, he sat up and looked around the room. Where was his Cordisa? Closing his eyes, he searched for his other half and absorbed from her all that had happened while he had been in a healing sleep. What he discovered made him growl and push to her that he was going to seriously spank her ass! She had Sameth leave him asleep on purpose!

Then as he healed, she had run all over his ship talking to his warriors, asking questions from everyone, about life on their planet, how to run his ship and everything under the sun. She was a menace that he needed to discipline; she needed to learn how to show the proper respect to a warrior. Her place was by his healing body! She had met with captains from the other ships! She had tasked Sidhawk and Kirrek with bringing her mother to her. She was leaving a couple of ships to watch over her planet and so that the warriors could see if they could find their own Cordisa on her marble. She gave Loku his ship! Why? She had decided since the Goddess had such a feisty mate for his Second that he needed to be one of those tasked with protecting her planet until he found her. Where was he going? She had commandeered another ship's Captain to take them to his planet!

That was it. She was so going to get spanked for this. Concentrating on where she was at this moment, he found her in the Goddesses chapel talking to her as though she would pop in at any moment. Which he guessed was possible, as she had done that once before. Hailey did not realize how incredibly blessed she was to have spoken with her the one time. He pushed his anger at her for leaving him asleep to heal. She sent back a shrug, unconcerned for the proposed spanking.

She pushed his stupidity at him. The fact he had decided to give up, to just quit. Not even trying to fight for her and what they could be together, but making a decision to try to kill Varill or die by his hands. Without thinking of how the bond would try to force her to morph to him and try to save him. He had almost killed them both with his decision. How she was scared to love him this way and the entirety of her life to this point. She showed him everything at once in a tightly packed capsule that exploded inside his head. It physically rocked him back into the headboard. Her life had been horrible on so many levels. The only bright spot of her entire life was her mother and her best friend. Two women who loved her and she loved back with a devotion bordering on insanity. They had kept his fragile love together with either the unconditional love of a mother or a friendship that had been tested in the fires of pain and a mutual abuser.

Jarrek watched her life flow by in fast, painful memories. He saw how close he had come to never having known her at all. She was moments away from taking her life, before the Goddess had sent her mother to bring her back from the edge. He saw the days she had spent tending his body before going to watch how their daughter continued to grow at a rapid pace and how scared that made her. He watched her make decisions about her life, why she questioned everyone on board and why she had made the arbitrary decisions she knew that he would make if he were in the condition to do so. While he had been healing these last two weeks, she had been absorbing his life. How his life experiences had shaped him as a man and the future king of his planet. She had fallen in love all over again and now knew all the way to her marrow, he was perfect for her. Not necessarily perfect, he could still make her crazy and she knew she would drive him to pull his hair out, but that in the end, there was no one else who could complete her so perfectly.

He had tears forming in his eyes and spilling down his cheeks for the pain she had endured before he found her. He wanted to blow the little marble out of the sky, but knew she would not want that. He felt the love explode in his chest as he watched his daughter grow and develop. He could not wait to meet her and hold her in his arms. He wanted her mother more now, though.

He needed to hold her. Affirm that she was his, and real and forever his beloved.

Hailey wanted the same thing. She had quickly excused herself from the Goddesses room and made her way to Jarrek. He wanted to spank her and she had no objection at all. She wanted to do the same thing to him. She had worried for the first twelve hours, as it was touch and go for a moment. Then Jarrek had just, leveled out and began to heal. She said a very heartfelt thank you to the Goddess. She could feel her touch in Jarrek's recovery. She checked on the other earth woman, who, while healing, was still in a coma. Sameth could not figure out what was going on, but she explained to Sameth about traumatic situations that left a person in a comma while they dealt with what had happened. The human brain was a fascinating organ and their scientists still did not know all that the brain was capable of. It had eased his mind a little, but he watched her carefully. She was not his Cordisa either, she had inquired. So far, no one in the medical ward was her Corduva. That did not slow their devotion to her care. She was female and to be put first in all things. These warriors really believed it.

Absorbing Jarrek's life had been fascinating. It was as if she was watching a movie inside her head that went on and on, but you never had to hit pause to go to the bathroom or get dinner. It just continued to show her unless she told it to give her a break while she watched her daughter grow and develop. It was a fascinating process to see. She had often been pulled away or reprimanded, as she got lost in watching her daughter. Then they had forced her to eat and take care of herself. She tried to think of names for her daughter, but she hadn't found anything that just seemed perfect to her. She was hoping to get suggestions from her mom when she got here, which should be at any moment. She had sent Kirrek and Sidhawk to her planet to kidnap her momma five days ago. She knew it wouldn't be easy and had warned them both, but she figured they would learn about earth women soon enough. She had also told them to bring back lots of microwave popcorn. She already knew that watching her momma with these warriors was going to be so entertaining that she would kick herself if she didn't ask for the popcorn to watch the show.

The person she would miss the most was her best friend. She had given a long letter to Sidhawk and Kirrek to give to her friend, so that she knew that Hailey was alive, but she was off on an adventure of a lifetime. She offered her the chance to come with her on this journey, but couldn't see Grace taking her up on it. Well, her momma would come. She had not one doubt on that score, it's just she would want to pack the whole house to bring it with her. Momma of the big purse, because you never know just what you may need in any given situation. She wished for a moment that she had asked Sidhawk to video that meeting. It was sure to be entertaining. In fact, she may have to ask Jarrek to make that a decree. That any interaction with earth woman would have to be recorded. For historical purposes of course, not just for the entertainment factor. She could almost believe she meant that. No, she couldn't. It was just too funny how these warriors strived to understand the speech and slang.

Hailey walked into the room she shared with Jarrek, who immediately pinned her with a stare; hot enough to just about melt the clothes from her body. In a half of a second, she was wet and ready for whatever he wanted from her body.

"Cordisa." Jarrek growled at her in his thick, sexy brogue.

"Corduva." She answered his growl with a slow, slinky walk towards him, while reaching for the ties on her gown. Two tugs later, she was naked and Jarrek was eating her up with his eyes.

"I find myself with a small dilemma, my love." Jarrek rasped.

Running her hands down her chest, she circled her nipples as they tightened under his stare. "Hmm, that feels good. What dilemma would that be, my mate?" She asked and stopped at the end of the bed.

"You are in great need of a spanking, my dear. Yet, I want to sink myself inside you right away. I need you desperately. I want to reaffirm our bond." Jarrek told her.

"That is no dilemma, my love, as you may have me any way that you want me. Should I lie across your lap? Should I crawl up your body and lick my way up? I could always climb on and sink that thick cock deep inside me and ride us both to completion." She told him while continuing to pinch her nipples under his watchful eye. She started to run her hand down her stomach to play along her folds, but he growled and then pounced. For such a large man, he was very fast. He went from reclining against the bed to lunging forward to wrap his arms around her and turned so that she landed on her back on the bed, while her legs hung over the edge. She spread them wide as he dropped to his knees and attacked her pussy as though starving.

He gripped her hips in an almost punishing hold; he used tongue, lips and teeth to consume her pussy. She gripped his head in her hands and fisted them in his hair, unsure if she was going to pull him away so that he was a little gentler or if she was pushing his face in her cunt begging for more, harder, faster. It did not seem to matter to Jarrek, as he was feasting on her cunt the way that he wanted and was not going to be held back. She could hear the MINE that sang across their link and it caused shivers of need to swim in her veins. She was soaking his face in her juices and it was audible how wet her pussy was. It made small, squelching sounds as he feasted.

She felt no embarrassment over her bodies' reaction to him, she reveled in how he got her body to sing and respond to him. Jarrek nipped her clit with his teeth sending her straight over the edge screaming her orgasm. He gave her body no time to come down, as he got to his feet and picked her up at the same time, he slammed her cunt onto his cock in a fierce move that had her screaming again. Not in pain, but because she exulted his savagery, soaking his animalistic need for her and returning it. He held her as though she weighed nothing and slid her up and down his cock in hard, fast jabs. He was chanting his love to her along their link. How wonderful she felt on his cock, how much he loved her and would worship her body, how forever with her would only be the start of their love. Jarrek rammed her body on his shaft pulling her hips forward so that her clit hit his pelvic bone and sent pleasure through her body, tightening that core of tension and winding it tighter and tighter until she felt as though she would die when it burst in orgasm.

"Close, oh, so close. More please. Love you." She chanted to him between breaths, until she broke screaming his name and leaving long, deep gouges down his back from her nails. "Jarrek!"

Jarrek felt her pussy flutter and tighten on his cock, could feel along their bond that she was about to explode and pounded her a little harder and faster. He gave her what she needed to send her over, knowing that her pussy would tighten so much she would take him with her. When she dug her nails in his back and raked them down, the pain of her cutting into his skin caused his to break first. He was screaming his orgasm a second before it all burst for her and she came screaming his name. He hoped the fire on his back scarred. It would be an honor to carry the proof of how well he loved her on his body.

He staggered to the bed, lay back down, and pulled her on top of his body. He needed a minute to catch his breath. She made him strong, weak, dizzy, so in love and a million other emotions that he needed a moment to catch up. His breathing and hers began to even out before he could sort through his more prevalent emotions. Jarrek decided that he could not say how he felt. He could not come up with the correct words, or words that actually encompassed the depth and breadth of what he was feeling, so it would be easier to send them to her through their bond.

"I love you too, Jarrek. They just haven't invented a word that is large enough to hold what we feel for each other. I will love you for eternity comes the closest, and is nowhere near enough." She told him as he struggled to say what he felt.

"Yes, exactly jabir minka. I will strive to let you know I love you as often as possible." Jarrek said and then pulled her up his body so that he could nibble her neck and kiss her lips. He was just about to deepen the kiss when his comm chimed.

"I am going to disconnect that stupid thing. It always goes off when I want to make love to you." Jarrek complained.

She chuckled, but moved out of his hold and off the bed, saying, "Answer it. It may be that my momma is here. I sent Kirrek and Sid to get her. I can't wait to see her." She stood up to go to the cleanser. She didn't want to see her momma after such a long absence smelling of sex. No matter how good it was, it was just rude.

"You still earned yourself a spanking for all the orders that you have been throwing around here lately. You should have spent all of your time with me." Jarrek told her as he picked up the comm and shouted a "Speak" into the phone.

One minute later Jarrek walked into the cleanser as she was stepping out, pushing her back against the wall. "Well hello, handsome. Did you miss me?" Hailey said laughing and smiling up into Jarrek's face.

"Hmm. I did, but want your lips as I am cleansed. That was indeed your momma and they are requesting that both of us come at once. There seems to be some kind of problem down at the landing bay. Kirrek apparently stole some woman from your planet saying that she is his mate and Sidhawk's. Your Marti just found out that they kidnapped the other woman and is yelling at my brother, while hitting him with her big bag. Sidhawk, who is usually such a gentle soul, is holding this woman back from leaving and wandering the ship and they are both screaming your name."

"Shit! Hurry Jarrek, I have to go save them!" she yelled and pushed against his chest while trying to wiggle out of the enclosure.

"Relax little bird. I am finished. Dress and we will go now." Jarrek said to try keep his voice even, so that she would relax, but is was soon obvious that it was not working.

She rushed to her dress on the floor by the bed and pulled it up in a quick, impatient move. Another impatient motion and her sandals were on her feet. She turned to him ready to leave and he was still watching her, not even having put on his trousers.

"Hurry up, Jarrek. Don't make me leave you behind!" she threatened.

Jarrek gave her a stern look and said, "Do not. You are begging for a spanking Hailey and regardless of who is waiting I am about to give it to you."

"You are about to find yourself kicked in the balls, Jarrek. Do not condescend to me, right now. Dress quickly. It is rude to keep my momma waiting." Fluffing her hair into submission. Less than five minutes later, they walked into a scream-fest.

Jarrek took one look around, then threw back his head, and roared, "Enough!"

18.

The Perfect Way To Kill An

Argument

Everyone froze and Hailey had to laugh at the picture they all made. The usual personnel all stood around them gaping and laughing at the play enacted for their entertainment, right in front of them. There was her momma, with her arm cocked back ready to give Kirrek another good hit with her purse. Kirrek was looking down at her with his angry face and his arms crossed, as though her little bag was not in any danger of hurting him. Sidhawk stood with his back to us holding a shrieking termagant in his arms. He had moved her body to the side so that her legs had quit kicking him in the shins, and now dangled out behind him. The woman shrieked, "Bloody hell! Put me down you big red lummox!" and Hailey drew in her breath at the familiar curse. That was her best friend's ungodly shriek. "Grace! Momma!" Hailey cried out stepping further into the room. She was about to run to her momma and Grace, but Jarrek pulled her back against him.

"Wait one moment, little bird. Let us find out what is going on, first. Then we can welcome your family." Jarrek said into her hair, in a low enough voice that said it was just for her and along the bond he sent, "as the future Queen of Athria, let us be united on this, my dear."

Hailey paused for a moment and then stepped to Jarrek's side, so that they could approach the group together. She smiled at both of her momma's and Grace's expression of her mate. She sent a wink to Grace that left her silent and wide-eyed.

"Now, I would like you all to act like civilized adults and explain to me just what is going on." Jarrek said in his deep voice. I saw my momma's eyes widen at how deep and lovely his accent was and then glance to me next to him. I straightened my shoulders even more, for her perusal as, I didn't want to hear that a lady should stand straight and proud. I was proud to be standing next to Jarrek. I sent a big grin her way. She goggled at me as if she had never seen me smile in my life. I was going to harrumph at her, but that would earn another lecture on behavior that I didn't want to hear.

Helene straightened her own posture and took a step closer to us. "My name is Helene Edmondson; my daughter is by your side. I was asked by these men to come live with my daughter at her request. I was happy to do so. I thought that my daughter had died." She had to pause and clear her throat from the emotions even thinking about that had caused. I had to do the same hearing momma say those words, before she continued. "It took me a minute to get packed up and as they had a message that they were to deliver to Hailey's best friend Grace, I left them to do that. Well, I may have given a little advice on how to tell people that they were in a play about Satan's minions and were in costume if anyone stopped them. Then they left to go give her the message and I finished packing. I didn't see them again for hours. I just figured that they got lost. I was about to go out and try to find them, when they came back and asked if I was ready to go. Of course, I was not. No one with sense can ask a lady to be ready to pick up and move at a moment's notice. It is scandalous, sir. I held my temper though. I am a lady and advised them of that fact. When they offered to help me, it did go a mite faster. They are big strong men that you have Commander."

She leaned forward and whispered to her, "That is his brother, momma. Prince Kirrek."

"Really? Well I won't bow to him, Hailey. He is rude and uncouth. His daddy should have taken a strap to him on occasion. I am sure it would have helped his constitution."

Helene watched as her daughter held in her laughter and snuggled in to the huge red man beside her. She had never seen her look so happy. Why, she almost glowed with it. Focusing back on the issue at hand, she turned her gaze back to him and continued.

"They were both very solicitous on the way here, but it was always only one of them. When I first met them, that little one was always with Mr. Cranky. I could tell right away that they were a couple, in how they watched over one another. Then I only saw them one at a time on the way here. I minded my own business, but was curious why. Then when we get here, I see Kirrek with a woman slung over his shoulder like a sack of potatoes. She is kicking and hollering fit to wake the dead. Of course, when she started cursing I knew exactly who she was and tried to go to her rescue. Kirrek put her down at my request, but when I tried to keep Grace with me, they both objected quite fiercely! They both screamed in my face. Rude! They both need a good strapping."

"Brother," Kirrek began, but stopped at Jarrek's raised hand.

"I will hear from my new Marti, first brother. You may make your explanations to me next if you feel something needs to be clarified." Jarrek told Kirrek with a stern expression on his face. Hailey wondered if that was his "I am ruler" face and sent that question along their bond. His lips twitched into an almost smile, before he got control of it. He sent back his hand spanking her ass in hard, punishing swats. She blew a kiss up at him in front of his men and her momma. Jarrek wanted to grab up his beloved and lock them in a room so that he could follow up on that spanking with some long, deep strokes of his cock in her pussy. "Tease." He whispered down to her.

"Please continue, my new Marti." Jarrek asked Helene.

Helene wiped a non-existent piece of lint from her trousers and straightened her already perfect hair, before telling him, "Well. That was pretty much everything. Grace tried to escape, they both went to grab for her and I hit Kirrek with my bag to keep him away. She should have been able to evade the smaller one, but he has some skills. Too bad, for Grace. I was demanding your presence Hailey and telling Mr. Cranky Kirrek that he could not have Grace. She wasn't a pet of some sort that he could just kidnap and he and the other one both yelled out that she was their Cordisa, whatever that is." Helene finished.

Hailey sucked in a deep breath at that. Grace was a Cordisa to her brother-in-law and Sidhawk? Wow! "Grace, you lucky bitch! How did you get two, huh?" She hollered at her girlfriend and watched as Sidhawk set her on her feet, but pulled her back against his chest and wrapped his arms around her.

"Uh, Hailey. I don't even know what that means. I am not a lucky bitch, I am a kidnapped bitch!" Grace shrieked at her best friend. "They barely even packed my clothes. All of my favorite shoes and my coach purses were left behind! If that is not the most unlucky thing you have ever heard, I will kiss your but!" Grace wailed in her

British accent. It really was amazing that they were best friends when they were complete opposites. She was from Sussex originally, while Hailey was a dyed in the wool country girl. Her mom was even strange as she reminded Grace of an old-time southern' belle of the cotton mansion. She just wanted to turn back the clock and go home.

"You will go nowhere woman. You are my and Sidhawk's Cordisa. It will be our privilege to care for you and protect you and our young." Kirrek started lecturing Grace. Hailey actually winced when he started. Sidhawk was about to lose the hearing on that side if he wasn't careful with what he said to her. She could see Grace suck in her breath for an academy winning shriek, but thank Goddess she was interrupted by Loku on the intercom.

"My Prince, I am sorry to bother you at such an entertaining moment, but I thought you may like to know that you and your Cordisa are about to be Colti."

"Oh Jarrek, let's hurry. I want to be right there." Hailey was about to jump out of her skin she was so happy right then, and it was the perfect way to kill an argument. Turning to her Momma and her best friend in the whole universe, she asked them, "Would you like to meet my daughter? She is going to be born right now." Then smiled as their mouths dropped open in shock.

Epilogue

Hailey held her daughter close to her heart and smiled down at her perfect face. "Look at you. You are just the prettiest little angel that was ever born. You are so perfect and momma loves you, yes she does." She spoke down to her sleeping daughter. She had not opened her eyes yet, which according to Second Senior Medical Doctor Krases B'el Whalekin – in charge of her beautiful daughter's care was normal for a child born of an artificial womb. He tried to explain the science to her, but her eyes literally started to cross and glaze over, so he skipped the explanation on it and just told her what she really wanted to know. That her daughter was healthy and the Krakill had done nothing to harm her in any way.

She had pale red skin. A pale shade of pastel red. She had her daddy's black hair, but it was thick and curly like hers. She had a little rosebud of a mouth and the cutest button nose. She knew that her daughter would continue to grow and her facial features would grow and change, but she was the perfect mix of her and Jarrek.

She was currently surrounded by Jarrek, her momma, Grace, Sidhawk and Kirrek. Jarrek stood behind her and helped surround her and the baby in the protection of his love. While smiling down upon his personal little miracle as he kept calling her. "We need to consider names, my love." She told Jarrek.

"Do you have any that you have thought you might like to name her?" Sidhawk asked her.

"No. I have thought of many names, but was waiting for momma to get here to talk to her, and ask her opinion. I just couldn't make up my mind. I thought of Destiny, Hope, Zyana and Laria after Jarrek and Kirrek's momma. I am hoping that Jarrek will have some suggestions, like other girl names from his planet. Then I could kind of see what she reacted to and let her choose on her own." She answered, still not taking her eyes off the little bundle of love in her arms.

"Zyana is a word in our language little bird. It means wonder, a miracle or other cause of intense admiration or awe. I think that name is a perfect fit to our own little wonder," Jarrek said.

Helene leaned down and kissed her first grandbaby on the head. She was so happy she could barely contain it. That her daughter was so happy and had now given her this perfect little angel, she felt as if this was the reward. Kirrek and Sidhawk had explained that she would want for nothing and would no longer have to scrape to get by. Her daughter was to be the Queen of their planet, to rule at his side. Her biggest worry would be what to play with the newest Princess of Athria and trying to learn her new language. Although with their translators, they would understand her just fine and would soon learn her language, so the entire planet would be able to speak English as well.

She desperately wanted to hear the story of what had happened to her daughter and the adventure that she had been on, but for now was content with the fact that her daughter was alive, happy and a new mother. She did not care that her new son was a giant red man with a Mohawk, or that he was from another galaxy entirely. The glow to Hailey's cheeks was a remarkable improvement. Stepping back, she looked to Jarrek and said, "I realize the new parents will wish to spend time with their daughter so if someone can show me to my quarters and steer me to someplace to get something to eat, I will check back in with you tomorrow. I want to get settled in and then I will want to hear all about this adventure Hailey has been on."

Jarrek looked up from the perfect face of Zyana and answered his Marti. "Let me call one of my warriors who will be your guard while we are on this ship. They will be temporary quarters as we will be moving ships soon, so that I can take Hailey and Zyana to Athria. Space is no place to raise a family." Running a finger down Zyana's cheek, he kissed Hailey's head and went to the comm unit, and gave his orders. Stepping back to his family, he went back to watching Zyana sleep against Hailey's breast. Only when a warrior stepped to his side and cleared his throat did he raise his head again.

"Titus, I want you to meet Helene. She is my new Marti through Hailey. Please show her to her quarters, I have put her three down from my own. You are to be her personal guard while we are aboard ship. Show her how the prep stations work. Her luggage should already be in the room, so show her how to operate the closets and anything else she needs to know." Jarrek told him.

Hailey looked up and smiled at Titus saying, "Don't forget the cleanser unit. I had a hard time figuring out the waste disposer, as well, as how to operate the hand and body cleansers you have. If it were not for

Sidhawk, I would have embarrassed myself." She laughed and shook her head at the memory of trying to figure it out on her own and how she had scared herself thinking she was going to push a button and be sucked into space. "Good night, momma. I am so glad you are here. I promise that I will tell you everything tomorrow." She promised and then leaned over to kiss her momma's cheek.

Hailey watched her momma leave before turning serious eyes to Kirrek, Sidhawk and Grace, who would not let either man touch her. "Sidhawk I am so disappointed in you. Kirrek does stupid all the time from what you told me, but I explained my life to you on Earth and you still let him abduct Grace?" she told him. "If I did not have my hands full of this baby, I would have to hit you over the head with something very heavy."

"Hailey, I do not think you realize the seriousness of what happens to us when we find our Cordisa. We are physically incapable of allowing her to disappear or escape us. We must hold her, touch her, and take her somewhere safe so that we can bond her. That my mate and Kirrek's is the same person is a little bit of a surprise, as that only happens in cases of twins like Heathrick and Shemrick. They must share a mate. It has something to do with the parasite that inhabits them as embryos. There is scientific explanations, but I do not really know what they are as I am not a twin so had no need to be informed. Kirrek and I share a love bond and have for a thousand years, but" Sidhawk tried to explain, but was cut off by his Cordisa's high shriek of, "how long?" He was going to turn to her and explain to her the same as he had explained to Hailey, but she held him off. She resettled Zyana, who had fussed, disturbed by Grace's high pitch.

"Hush, Grace. The baby doesn't like your tone," and to Sidhawk, "I got this one Sid. I will talk to her about symbiot's and the age of your people and the history of the planet, a little later. Right now, I need to know, what is supposed to happen now?" Hailey asked and looked up to Jarrek.

"Hailey love, have you lost your damn mind looking to a man for an answer? What the hell happened to you?" Grace protested. Looking to a man for answers never helped a woman get anywhere in life. Make your own way and take shit from no one. This way if things go skitters, you had no one to blame, but yourself. Both she and Hailey had subscribed to this philosophy for quite some time.

"I think you are soon to find out, my friend. For now, can we both agree that we are all tired and need a nap before conquering the next problem?" she asked Grace and leaned a little more heavily against Jarrek.

"Yeah, sure luv. I know that being a new mum will exhaust you, but I want my own room." Grace demanded.

"For tonight I will agree to that. I will not return you to Earth. I know that you do not understand what has happened to you, I will let you sit down with Hailey tomorrow, she can share her story, and you can share yours. Accept that you are now Athrian, as that is what you became the moment my brother took you." Jarrek told her and then told Kirrek and Sidhawk to escort her to a room for the night and they would revisit everything the next day.

Hailey was a little apprehensive about Jarrek's decree to Grace, as she knew that Grace was not going to take something like that lying down. She would see it as a challenge to do her best to get back to Earth. "Jarrek are you sure you should let them take her to a room?" she began before Jarrek stopped her.

"Hailey I can feel your anxiety over this. I will put a guard on her door so that they cannot bother her for tonight, and then you can talk to her tomorrow. For now, let us retire to our room and put Zyana to bed before her next feeding. How is that shot working?" He asked Hailey as he began steering her to their rooms. Hailey had been given a shot that would have her milk come in, as she was worried that the baby would need her milk to survive. They had had no children for thousands of years and so she was accurate that they did not have the necessary ingredients to feed a baby. They would have been able to manufacture something approximating a mother's milk, but from the source was always preferred.

"I think it is working. My breasts are very tender and full right now. I actually want to get to our room to remove this gown. It is starting to restrict my movements and is becoming a little painful." she told him.

"You should have told me right away, little bird. I would have thrown them all out right away. Nothing is more important than you and Zyana. If you need a moment to get comfortable, then they can wait for you." Jarrek told her seriously, giving her a small reprimand with a low voice so as not to disturb his daughter.

Tomorrow would bring a new set of problems, but for now, Jarrek and Hailey were happy together, and enjoying the miracle that was Zyana. The rest of the world could pause for a moment while he enjoyed his Goddess given gifts, and if they did not want to wait, he would kill them and then go back to enjoying this time. He was going to have Hailey put Zyana down for a little nap while he showed her just how much he loved her and how happy he was that she had accepted him. His people were looking at an answered prayer when they looked at Hailey. She was everything he had ever desired and more that he did not realize he had needed in his life. After fourteen hundred and fifty years, he let the peace of this moment wash over him. It left him feeling humbled and so in love. He sent his desire for her pulsing through the link and felt her answering desire shoot back into him. He would spend a lifetime worshipping her, giving her his passion and Goddess willing more Cordisa's for his people.

Annikatalamenaria, Goddess of All Life, or Annika to Hailey watched from her plane of existence, while some of her devoted followers fed her little snacks and brushed her hair. She watched as Jarrek and Hailey made love and heard Jarrek's final thought, before he slipped into slumber. It was a prayer sent out by many of those onboard the ships just outside of Pluto in

Hailey's galaxy. She could only laugh as she replied, "Careful what you wish for, you may just get it, and it will sock you in the nose!" She had plans for the Athrians. They would thrive as a people once again. Well, only if they are able to convince their Cordisa's to have them. She was a Goddess, but even that was beyond her purview…

LANGUAGE LEXICON

Ansis – year

Colti - Parents

Cordisa – (feminine) heart's fate; beloved

Corduva – (masculine) heart's fate; beloved

Cruvek – equivalent to the curse word on earth of "Bastard"

Dek – hour

Domu - equivalent to earth curse word of "damn"

Faval – wait; stop

Jabir – bird

Jabir minka – my little bird

Marc – week

Marteo – (feminine) bonded mate and mother; wife

Marti – Mom; Mommy; Mother

Microsec – ½ of a second

Luzarian Worm – a slimy worm that emits a flatulence sound and secretes an ugly yellow puss that is extracted to help mix in with high dollar cleansing oils on several trading posts in the Elite Moons Luzarian Quadrant of space, as well as highborn households in the Ruzario Quadrant of the Nineteen moons sector . Highly valuable trade item, a rare but sturdy animal, that is not easily harmed.

Parasec – ¼ of a second

Prati – Dad; Daddy; Father

Pimba – a four foot tall domesticated cat that looks like the earth animal of cougar. Coloring can range from pale yellow to black and a brindle color. Can weigh up to 260 lbs.

Prateo – (masculine) bonded mate and protector; husband

Sec – second

Sect – day

Shivak loch croin – equivalent to the curse word on earth of "Son of a Bitch"

Versis – month

Verl – minute

Zilenta – A large spotted animal much like the earth animal panther, with the exception of spines around the rough of the neck. These spines can become raised if the zilenta feels in danger and will ooze a toxin that will paralyze its victim, giving it time to escape. Sometimes kept as pets as they are a wilder version of the Pimba, to which they are related.

Zyana – wonder, a miracle or other cause of intense admiration or awe.